Beyond My Words

Book 1

For anyone who's ever experienced pain at the hand of another. You're not alone.

Beyond My Words

A Novel by

Chandler R. Williamson

ISBN: 9798608496172

Printed in the United States of America

Contents

Part 1

The Writer

Prologue

Wind from his wings blasted back the needles of nearby pine trees when he landed in the clearing. The hunters' cries for justice faded into the night, bringing the assurance that he'd lost them. His sigh of relief burst from his nostrils in flames the color of the setting sun.

He surveyed his surroundings, trying to figure out exactly where he'd landed. They'd never chased him that far into the forest before. Each tree felt unfamiliar as he backed into them, hoping for shelter from the open air. Their branches bent from the impact of his entrance and a flash of embarrassment rumbled with a purr in his throat.

For the first time in several hours, his thoughts wandered. The hunters had never been so persistent and angry before. What had he done to deserve the arrows that whizzed past his wings?

Sunlight peeked through the canopy of trees.

Morning, he mused, closing his eyes and resigning himself to the change once again.

Magic tingled in his talons and circled up his legs, wrapping around each scale and scattering into the air in a puff smoke the shade of lavenders. The candy-like smoke sweetened his taste buds before the tingling sensations enveloped his whole body and turned the world black for an instant.

Her voice came to him again . . . beckoning in an alluring tone. Whispering his name. She seemed dangerous. Tantalizing. Yet, he found himself drawn to her in spite of himself. She sounded beautiful. He'd never seen the lady behind the voice, but her song comforted him through the change.

He opened his eyes again to a world vibrant with colors other than the silvery-red tint of the world he saw through the eyes of a dragon.

The vibrant leaves welcomed a fresh morning where he found himself lying in a heap of leaves and dirt. He often awoke this way. Blinking away the haze of sleepless rest, he surveyed the clearing, taken aback by its unfamiliarity. He sat up, muscles groaning and sore from the change from dragon to man.

"Gah," he gasped, gripping a spot in the center of his spine and finally realizing how far he'd strayed from the palace.

The vast forest swallowed the world beyond its thick pine trees and aspens. Something seemed odd about these trees. They clumped together as if hiding something. His eyes scanned down the long line of pines, stretching as far as he could see.

They formed a wall, too thick to see through to the other side, their branches only allowing tiny peeks into the world beyond it.

A few paces away, an ancient looking aspen had fallen, its thick trunk uprooted on his side of the forest and smashed between two of the pines. Limping past the soreness in his knees and brushing off branches, dirt, and leaves from his tunic, he approached it, using its trunk as a sort of crutch. Part of the aspen jutted into the air on the other side. He couldn't see another way around climbing onto the tree and walking across it like a tightrope.

Shaking off his tense limbs, he hoisted himself onto the tree, pushing away pine needles away with a wince. Nothing looked too different on the other side.

He hopped onto the ground, instantly encompassed in the same magic that changed him into a dragon every night. When he opened his eyes again, his tunic and knickers had been replaced with strange clothing that hugged his body too tightly. The course fabric of his trousers felt foreign and uncomfortable. The sleek shirt felt smooth in contrast, but still foreign and strange.

He hadn't seen magic outside of his own curse since it was cast.

Curiosity slid a grin across his face with the promise of adventure.

Chapter 1

"Scales itched his skin as they crawled quickly across the back of his hand. He was changing again."

~ Ellie's Story

Words fell recklessly onto my notebook's pages, bending and swaying against each other with every graceful stroke of my pen. I hungered for more, trying to hold myself back long enough for my hand to keep up with my imagination. Intoxicated by their spell, I watched each word appear, smearing beauty across the pages. Every piece of it enthralled me.

I couldn't stop. I let myself be carried away by them . . . Until hands covered my face, blocking my vision of the words following my pen on paper. I flinched as Brock laughed behind me.

"Brock," I scolded, my smile seeping through as I pushed him away with an elbow in the ribs. "Isn't that getting a little old?"

"Never. You're totally asking for it."

Hugging my notebook across my chest and leering playfully at him, I leaned against the locker beside me. "How so?"

"You were so focused on that notebook." He flung an apple from his backpack and chomped. "It's my responsibility to drag you back into reality. I'm doing you a favor, Ellie."

I nearly had to dodge the chewed-up apple peel launching from his lip and onto the floor.

Turning toward the crowd in search of Jennica, I shook my head. "You've done it since the fourth grade," I retorted, pulling my bag higher onto my shoulder and shutting my locker.

"Like I said, you need rescuing," he said, biting his apple again and running his fingers through his spikey, blonde hair.

I turned back to him, subconsciously describing his stance.

He leaned against the lockers beside me, emerald eyes scanning the crowd of teenagers. One leg crossed over the other and rested on the tip of his Converse shoe.

My focus vaguely wandered to the words *"Taylor's Grove Archery Team"* strewn across the chest in chipped letters and I smiled to myself. He'd worn that nearly every day since freshman year when he joined the school's team. Small holes dotted the hoodie from the bleach his sister spilled on it. Brock swore it gave him some sort of superpower during archery tournaments.

"Well, I guess I should thank you for saving the damsel in distress from her stupor of thought. Keep in mind though that you're interrupting a writer at work and she could write you into the story. That could end very badly for you."

"You love me too much to do that," he scoffed, glancing warily at me.

"Try me," I played, knowing he was right. I'd never really have the heart to kill off a character to spite him.

The bell rang, demanding my full attention with its persistent screeching. Shutting my locker, I tucked away the handcrafted notebook Dad made for me into my purple shoulder bag.

"Where's Jennica?" Brock moaned, exasperated. "My mom's making lasagna tonight and I'm starving."

I turned back to the crowd. "Knowing Jennica, she's probably with Jason."

Brock rolled his eyes. "Typical. Let's go."

He dragged me into the crowd, towing me behind him in the flow of teenagers heading for the buses outside. I hated when he forced his way into crowds like that, especially when he dragged me behind him. I cringed away from the shoulders and elbows shoving past me, trying to hold onto Brock's hand for my life. The world felt smaller cramped between hot, sweaty bodies and I couldn't help but cringe and try hiding from it. I closed my eyes, trying to distract myself until I could breathe properly. The only way I knew how to do that was letting words weave into my thoughts. Then, I could relax a bit more.

Immediately, I missed my writing solitude. My fingertips tingled with words yearning to be released onto paper.

I had to get that idea down before I forgot it and I couldn't forget it until I wrote it down. I longed to escape my reality for the short period of time when I could see beyond my words on the paper and through new eyes with my characters.

Later, Ellie. It can wait.

At last, we reached the foyer and I rushed out of the crowd and relaxed against the stone wall, breathing like I'd run a marathon. Apparently, I'd held my breath all the way down the hall.

I glanced out the window at the buses. Relieved, I sighed, glad I didn't have to endure the bus anymore. Monika's hand-me-down, piece of junk Nissan was now *my* piece of junk. If it kept me off the bus, I *loved* it.

His wings beat against the night.

The words teased me with my inability to write them down.

I tried to smile at people when they passed us because of something Dad told me as a little girl. "*The smile of a stranger could save someone's life.*" Sometimes, he reminded me of a fortune cookie. Smiling was hard when I could hardly hear anything past the nagging muse pulsing inspiration through me like a current.

Tumbling through the air, he breathed a sigh that lit the night sky with flames. They kissed his scales, calming his nerves of the hunters searching for him.

I looked back down at my notebook, running my fingertips along the bumpy texture of the scarlet dragon engraved on its cover. Its long, thin body wrapped around the stem of a crimson rose, glistening in the lights above me and giving the illusion of scales.

I could almost see that dragon soaring across a moonlit sky as he watched his kingdom sleeping below.

Dad designed the cover himself, basing it off the stories he told me as a little girl.

My shoulders sagged with the reminder of what day it was. He'd been gone for five years to the day. Though I hadn't seen him since he blew me a kiss before his disappearance, I still didn't want to believe he was truly gone.

I shut my eyes, letting in a slow breath, the musty-sweet smell of old paper wafted from my notebook, helping me remember how he smelled the last time I saw him. The day Dad gave it to me when I was fifteen.

"You okay, Ellie?" Brock asked.

I flinched, forgetting him beside me. My focus flashed to him for an instant and I smiled unenthusiastically.

"Yeah, I'm fine," I said too quickly.

He smirked, wrapping me in a side-hug. Brock rarely showed that level of empathy, so I had to relish in it as long as I could, hugging him back.

Something about reciprocating Brock's embrace brought out emotion in me I hadn't recognized that whole day. He knew what today meant to me. Dad disappeared five years ago. Almost up to the hour.

Sniffing, I pulled away from him and swiped at tears that'd slipped through without me realizing. Brock's mouth pressed together and he stepped back, leaning against the rough stone wall beside me.

I silently watched the puddles in the parking lot ripple with the constant flow of droplets. A gray haze hovered near the ground and gave a uniquely calming, yet eerie, appearance to the world.

How could I describe the way the air smelled?

Sweaty teenagers crammed into one, tight space, making the atmosphere feel thick and stuffy.

Not worth the effort. What else is there?

My mind turned toward the pitter-patter of raindrops and I smiled.

I loved the sound of rain.

Dad always said that each raindrop had its own story. When they hit the roof, they told it to you. He told me to listen closely whenever it rained and maybe I'd learn something new.

The memory made me chuckle. Even though they were only childish fairytales made up in his over-active imagination, I missed his stories. They gave me a sense of innocence that disappeared with him.

With another sniff, I pushed my sandy blonde hair from my eyes and stood taller to search for Jennica again. Taylor's Grove wasn't big, yet it seemed to have an overwhelming number of citizens.

Finally, she approached with her head of loosely curled, auburn locks down, thumbs flying across the phone in her hands.

She was lucky every guy in school waited in a mile-long line to impress her. She hardly ever opened a door herself.

Not bothering to acknowledge Lucas, a short boy with glasses and brown hair, she kept her head down while he held the door for her. He watched her walk away, gawking with a dazed expression. I felt bad for him. Jennica could be harsh when she wasn't interested.

She kept walking with her head down, traveling straight for the glass doors to the outside.

"Jenna," I hollered, almost too late.

Flipping her hair, she halted, staring at the door with wide eyes. She turned to me and Brock, letting her head fall down again to finish her text, her frilly, blue skirt swaying around her thighs as she walked.

"Thanks, Ellie," she said, placing a hand on my arm. "Could've died there."

"Did you even notice Lucas open the door for you?" I asked, gesturing to the boy still swooning.

"Hmm?" She glanced before waving a dismissive hand at him. "Oh, yeah. But if I give him the time of day, he'll be all over me. Some guys just don't know how to take a hint unless I make it painfully obvious. Hold my bag, loser." She shrugged off her shoulder bag, tossing it at Brock as she slipped her arms through the sleeves of her white, designer jacket.

I turned to Brock sympathetically, who rolled his eyes, tossing on his hood.

"Loser?" I asked Jennica, giving her a look. "Do you have to be so mean about it?"

She blinked, but shook her head, laughing under her breath. "Yes."

Lucas rushed to open the door for her again. She walked past him, barely acknowledging the gesture as she pushed her way outside.

His chivalry toward her reminded me of Erick in my writing when he wanted to impress a girl. His regularly chivalrous nature amplified by his want to impress.

I sighed, feeling sorry for Lucas. I approached him, lightly touching his shoulder as we passed. "Thank you, Lucas. That was sweet of you."

I glanced at Brock whose mouth lifted to one side in a smile that usually made me feel more relaxed. However, his fixed gaze made my skin tingle with a sense of being watched.

"What?" I asked, rubbing at goosebumps on my arms.

"Nothing," he replied. "I just like that side of you."

I hesitated, unsure what he referred to. I was just being nice where Jennica was rude. Brock wrapped his arm around my shoulders, shaking me affectionately as we walked out of the school. I laughed, patting his back. Jennica had already made it to my car, glaring at us as we approached my hand-me-down Nissan.

"It's about time," she snapped. "My hair's soaked."

I fought back my chuckle at Jennica's priorities while messing with the faulty locks.

"Sorry, Jenn. But you should've waited for us—Curse these stupid locks," I yelped before the key finally turned and we all threw open our doors and got in.

Brock shook his hair all over the upholstery, shivering dramatically. "Now *that* is what I call getting pelted by raindrops. What a rush."

I pursed my lips at the droplets of rainwater soaking my gearshift and dashboard from his hair and hoodie.

Classy, Brock.

"Thank you for shaking your soaking wet hair all over my car," I said sarcastically as I backed out.

"Sorry," Brock said passively, shrugging off his hoodie and tossing it onto Jennica's lap behind him. She flinched and threw it to the other side of the car like a dirty rag.

"Thanks again," I said.

"You're welcome." His wide, cheesy grin made me laugh as I shook my head.

"Brock, this thing stinks." Jennica griped. "Why did you throw it back here with me?"

Brock exhaled deeply, reclining his chair to eliminate Jennica's legroom. "I knew it would irritate you."

She groaned and scooted to the middle seat. "You're disgusting," she muttered, holding up her hands in surrender. "If you'd shower more, maybe this wouldn't be so . . ."

Their banter faded to the background and my thoughts wandered, gliding with words, descriptions, and dialogue between different characters in my story again.

This time, I imagined a scene with Erick and his cousin as the transition between man and dragon began. He held Erick as he lay dying, the red dragon he'd been cursed to become in the moonlight taking over forever.

"Don't leave me here," he shouted, anger seething into his tone the louder his voice grew. "You can't die like this. Tyral needs you."

Erick's eyes felt heavy as the pain numbed his stomach with a deep burn that'd never accompanied the change before.

"Ellie," Brock screeched.

Instinctively, I slammed on my brakes, my heart pounding. The stop sign to the right of the road mocked me with the adrenaline pulsing through me. Soon followed by embarrassment.

"Sorry," I whimpered, pressing my hand against my heart.

Car rides provided me with ample time to contemplate different plotlines and twists. It'd proved to be more of a curse since I often found myself unable to focus on real conversations through the ones happening in my thoughts.

Thankfully, traffic was sparce in Taylor's Grove. So at least my wandering mind wasn't usually a physical hazard. Just a social one.

"Thinking about writing again?" Jennica asked, exasperated.

I felt myself blush, hanging my head in shame. "Yes."

Brock laughed, though it sounded more like a cough. "Oh, Ellie."

I sighed, knowing they thought I was crazy. "I was thinking of the ending of my story again," I said as if that were an excuse for nearly running a stop sign. "I think I've finally figured out how it really feels for him when he's dying."

Brock shook his head with a playful grin. "If anyone else said something like that, I'd call the cops."

"Ellie, maybe you shouldn't talk so openly about your characters like they're real people. It's a little off-putting sometimes," Jennica suggested, judgement in her tone hiding under concern. "Sometimes, I wish you'd think about something else. Like dating."

Sighing, I started on the road again. "You know, I could kill you with a pen and paper too in the form of those fictitious characters. That's what happened with Mikey. So be careful what you wish for."

The car fell silent again after that and my mind ran away from me again as I drove down the winding road toward Jennica's house.

The dense forest constantly surrounding our little town gave me inspiration I couldn't quite explain. If I could've lived forever in their magical oasis of security and mystery, I would've.

Sometimes, I'd drive into the mountain roads outside of town to think and escape human companionship to breathe the new air I only found with my one, true love.

Words.

Chapter 2

"Moonlight peeked from behind the canopy of trees overhead."

~ Ellie's Story

Alone at last," I breathed after Brock left my car and sprinted to his house. I loved my friends more than anyone and loved spending time with them, but I lived for the time I got alone after school. It was a time for me to revive myself and focus my attention to what mattered most to me.

Shifting my car into gear, I backed out of his driveway and drove to the only local bookstore in Taylor's Grove.

I spent nearly two hours there every day after dropping them off, writing and reading in a place where I could be alone with the joyful solitude of words on pages. People didn't often disturb me there and the bookkeepers all knew me from elementary. Dad and I would race each other to see who could find the books with the most interesting cover or title.

The quiet walls of the bookstore became my sanctuary after he disappeared. I still remembered the feeling when the police dismissed our missing person report as nothing more than abandonment, telling us they had *"more important"* things to do.

My fingers gripped tightly to the steering wheel and I breathed deeply, trying not to be angry about it. No good would come from that.

Besides, I was about to spend the next two hours in a place where I knew no one would ever disappoint or leave me.

Erick grimaced, knowing his transformation would begin soon as he gazed into the light of a full moon. Those nights were the hardest.

I wrote that a long time ago, but the words still seemed delicious to me. My fingers twitched to write what I'd imagined earlier. I'd been trying to figure out how it felt for Erick when his curse to become a dragon finally killed him.

Now, I had it. And I couldn't wait to write it down.

When I reached the bookstore, relief swept over me with a sigh as I grabbed my bag and tossed open my car door. The rain subsided some, leaving small sprinkles of droplets glistening on my eyelashes. I grinned up at the sky before entering writer's holy ground.

The familiar scent of old books left my senses elated and anxious to explore new worlds of possibilities and wonder. Rita, the bookkeeper at the front desk, greeted me and I smiled back at her.

I headed straight for my usual table in the fiction section.

The building had been there since before I was born. Vaguely, I wondered what it would be like to host a book signing there. The passing daydream left a lingering smile in its wake.

Dad told me about when he would go there in search of a new story. He'd always find something new, even though the scarce selection dulled in comparison to others I'd seen in pictures.

Only seven sections filled the whole store. Fiction, nonfiction, audio CDs, audiobooks, children's, young adult, and adult. The audio section only consisted of one small section with four rows on each cherry wood shelf.

Sometimes, I wished for more. I'd seen pictures on the internet of bookstores and libraries around the world filled to the brim with countless books. Each of those books held thousands upon thousands of stories, just waiting to be discovered, devoured by hungry readers all over the world.

I yearned to see them one day.

Once I'd settled into the cushioned chair, I flipped through my notebook and started writing.

I knew Jennica was right. I knew my characters weren't real. I knew I'd never actually meet Erick or fly through the air like his dragon form like I got to in my writing, but I still trusted him with my heart and soul. He'd been there for me when no one else was. When life hit hard, he was there to remind me of the good in the world. Though I'd never meet him, Erick was more real to me than anything had ever been before.

Unlike real people, my characters would always be there for me when I needed them. I could live out my romantic, adventurous fantasies through them without any fear of having them turn their backs on me or let me down. I could always rely on them to catch me when I fell.

His cousin's voice faded in and out. Suddenly, a shock of what felt like fire shot through him, seeming to poison his blood with its powerful blow.

Words flowed from me like butter off a warm biscuit. I loved how clearly my imagination saw each scene unfold before me as if it were through my own eyes. My heart leaped in my chest with anticipation of what words would come next, each one making me crave more.

Erick's body writhed. He might've screamed from the sharp and intense burning shocking his bloodstream, but he didn't care. He only wanted it to end. His body fell against the forest floor, exhausted as he prayed for the mercy of an end.

"Excuse me."

I only half-noticed the voice blending with words on the page. Realizing someone had spoken to me, I paused. I knew that voice. . .

Blinking through my haze of creativity, I looked up to see a guy standing by my table, double-taking to gawk at him.

I recognized him instantly, but I'd never seen him before. At least not . . . here.

Strands of sleek, black hair rested on his forehead in different directions without much of an indication as to where they were supposed to rest naturally. A few waves intertwined with his straight locks that grew to the base of his neck. His dark eyebrows, dominant on his face, made his eyes stand out more. A thin layer of whiskers grew below his chin and under his bottom lip, stubble lining his nicely squared jaw.

I tilted my head, glancing back at my notebook in confusion before meeting his gaze again. I expected him to disappear into my notebook when I looked back up. He still stood there, his expression confident, yet a little uncomfortable.

The world slowed as I stared into his eyes, so blue they were almost silver. No. They actually *were* silver.

How is that possible? I've never actually met anyone with silver eyes before.

That should've taken me by surprise, but I knew them like a vivid memory from a dream.

He looked incredibly like . . .

"Hello," he said, his voice deep and masculine as he flashed a smile that made my heart skip a beat. A crinkle in his cheek gave it just the right amount of charm.

I swallowed. "Hey."

"Um . . . I hope you don't mind my intrusion." A slight accent blended his consonants together. "What are you writing?"

Self-conscious, I snapped my notebook shut and tucked it under the table. "Nothing."

He stared at me a second before laughing nervously. "Alright, I apologize. A bit too forward of an approach," he muttered. "Do you mind if I join you?"

I hesitated. The idea of writing in front of an audience made me shift with discomfort. I knew he probably wouldn't be able to read over my shoulder, yet I still felt scrutinized and judged. What if he made fun of me for the way I held my pen between my index and middle finger? Or the weird faces I pulled while deep in thought? I didn't even have an excuse for why I did it. I'd always just done it that way.

My eyes scanned his appearance again.

Guys who looked like him usually didn't pay much attention to me because Jennica usually pounced on them too quickly for them to notice the quiet observer beside her.

What did this guy want?

Out of curiosity more than anything, I resigned myself to ending my writing session for the time being and gestured to the seat across from me.

"S—sure, go ahead."

You better be worth it. I'm giving up writing time for this.

He flashed another smile, teasing me with a hint of perfect teeth.

"Thank you," he said, inclining his head slightly in a bow as he sat, leaning his elbows on the table. "So, what *were* you writing?" Gesturing to my notebook, he eyed me, examining my expression like he anticipated a specific response.

I squinted at him, my spine stiffening with skepticism.

"Haven't I already answered that question?" It came out less like a genuine inquiry and more like a snappy accusation. I cringed. "It's nothing."

He chuckled lightly, drumming his fingers on the table. "If it was nothing, you wouldn't have hidden it so quickly."

I blushed. I'd been caught. It didn't really seem like his business anyway.

"Why do you want to know?"

I winced at the memory of the last time I showed my story to someone other than Brock or Jennica after Dad disappeared. That ended in mocking laughter and a reputation for having such a stupid imagination. After that, I decided it would be best to wait until I was at least old enough to start submitting queries to editors and literary agents.

He swallowed and his eyes widened, voice cracking slightly. "I may have an . . . investment in it."

I pulled back, unsure what to make of that. He was definitely hiding something.

"Are you an editor?" I asked, placing the notebook protectively on my lap and folding my arms in a closed-off gesture.

He shook his head, a guilty gleam in his eyes. "No."

"A publisher? Agent?"

He hesitated. "No."

"Then what kind of investment could you have in my story?"

He chuckled humorlessly and rubbed the back of his neck. I blushed when I noticed his bicep flex. I pretended fascination in a crack in the table in a futile attempt to hide that I'd noticed.

"I could've been simply making conversation," he observed.

"Oh," I muttered, feeling stupid for not considering that and getting so defensive over something so simple. Frowning, I played with a small centerpiece of red roses. "Sorry, I guess I'm a little too private about it." *That's an understatement.* "It's nothing special, just some stories I've had in my head since I was little."

He smiled with fun in his eyes as he tilted his head a bit and leaned his elbows on the table. I leaned away from him, unsettled by how his attention seemed consumed by me like nothing in the world compared to listening to me speak.

"I'd love to know more," he said, his voice low and smooth. "What's your name?"

Speaking of smooth. . .

Suddenly, my nerves tingled with anxiety as I gazed into those mesmerizing, silver eyes.

"Elizabeth Deeré," I blurted and quickly regretted it. *Why'd I use my full name?* "I mean, Ellie." *That's better.*

He chuckled softly, his mouth twitching into an amused grin. "You're cute, Ellie. May I at least see the cover?"

My mind scrambled, sticking stubbornly to his first words. *You're cute, Ellie.* Not many guys told me I was cute. Pretty, maybe. But never cute. In spite of myself, I smiled, feeling my cheeks burn with the compliment.

What would be so wrong with showing him the cover? It wouldn't make a difference either way. Jennica always told me to be less protective of the notebook. Even though Dad made it, it was just a book, after all.

Reluctant, I inhaled deeply and held it up for him to see.

His complexion went ghoulishly white and he leaned closer, a tremor shivering through him.

"Where'd you get that?"

"My dad. Why does that matter?"

He made no eye contact but stared blankly at the book, seeming suddenly lost in thought.

"It's you," he murmured thoughtfully. His brow knit together, bewilderment crossing his expression when he finally looked at me again. "It's *you?"* His tone shifted to more exasperated and almost irritated.

I didn't know what had changed. He seemed so calm and collected moments earlier. Now, he screamed unpredictability. Slowly, my hand reached for my keychain pepper spray, poised to use it if necessary.

"Yeah, it's me. Who are you?"

"*You're* the writer? You're so . . ."

I leered at him, silently daring him to finish that sentence.

"Young."

"Excuse me?" I snapped, offended by his underlying accusation. Just because I was young didn't mean I was incapable of—

"How old are you?" he continued, his eyes rolling over my appearance as if to somehow guess by simply looking at me. Instantly, I felt exposed and I tentatively touched the collar of my T-shirt.

"Eighteen."

His mouth opened as he gaped at me and he ran his fingers through his hair, groaning a lifeless laugh. "My life is in the hands of an eighteen-year-old," he mumbled.

I hesitated, unsure if I'd heard him right. I had to have misheard him somehow. Staring at him with uncomfortable fear rising into my stomach, I swallowed.

"*Excuse me?*" I demanded, quickly glancing at the bookkeeper, Rita. She thoughtfully arranged books on the shelves, hardly paying any attention to me.

When I looked back at him, a small smile had replaced the hopeless annoyance he'd worn before. He had a nice smile, charming and thoughtful as he gazed at me, though the sudden changes in his demeanor put me more on-edge by the second.

"I've been searching everywhere for you. I expected some wise, old sorcerer when I thought of the Great Writer. I guess it's better to find a pretty girl instead," he said confidently, though mostly to himself.

I froze beneath that look, completely mortified by it. "Great Writer? What are you talking about?"

His eyes searched my expression as he got up, sliding into the seat beside me. His arm glided across the back of my chair as he leaned close to me. I pulled away, stiff and afraid and not sure what to do.

"What if I told you that everything you wrote in that notebook came true? That everything in that story exists? Every character, world, and scene."

I twirled the pepper spray between my fingers, getting ready to shoot it into his eyes if he came any closer. Something in his silver eyes struck me. I might've imagined it, but the glimmer in his irises rippled like the scales of a lizard. I blinked quickly, trying to wake myself up. The effect didn't go away but seemed more noticeable.

It took a second for me to realize what he'd said. When it finally sunk in, a whirlwind of emotions flurried inside me at impressive speeds.

My story coming to life?

The thought made me want to cry. How many times was I going to be mocked for believing my characters were real people I could talk to? Mikey mocked me nearly every day for it, creating scenarios where he'd ridicule me in front of everyone, making me out to be crazy so he could feel better about himself. Dad was the only one who hadn't laughed at me at least once for believing that. Why today, of all days, did it have to happen again?

I went to the library as an escape from all the ridicule, not to jump into the belly of the beast.

Is this guy just another one of Mikey's loyal followers?

I scooted away from him, shaking my head and nearly falling off my chair.

"Who are you?" I asked, glaring.

"My name is Erick McKinley. I'm your character."

Chapter 3

"His monster yearned to escape, triggered by the fear burning through him with fire in his veins."

~ *Ellie's Story*

I stared at him, reciting those words in my head, trying to make sense of them together like that. His breath slowed, eyes anxious for my response. All at once, my heart turned cold and I loathed the sincerity in his tone and expression. He was serious. And a very good actor. If I was a stupid girl, I would've fallen for it.

"Very funny," I scoffed, rolling my eyes and leaning my elbow on the table. I still held onto the pepper spray, not shy about letting him know it was there. He barely seemed to notice.

"What is?"

"And now you're gonna tell me all about my character now, right? Pretend like you know everything by spewing out facts like his favorite color and what he wears to bed at night?"

He hesitated, pulling back a little as if he hadn't expected that response. "Well, if that would convince you, then I guess so."

"It won't." I stood, putting away my notebook and hoisting my bag onto my shoulder as I headed for the door.

"Wait, hold on."

He grabbed my arm before I could get too far. Instantly, I yanked it away, flipping around to find him standing right behind me. I glowered at him, pointing my finger at him like a dagger.

"*Don't* touch me. I don't know who you think you are, but no one can touch me without *my* permission. If Mikey put you up to this, tell him his plan backfired because I'm not falling for it. Not today."

He held up his hands in surrender of my intense response. "I'm sorry," he said, tentatively stepping away. "I'm only trying to save myself. Please just hear me out."

I hesitated. No one had said they were just trying to save themselves before. That piqued my interest and I felt myself soften a bit, curiosity overpowering my resolve as I tucked the pepper spray into my back pocket again. Folding my arms, I flipped my blonde hair aside and watched him skeptically.

"Alright then," I said. "I'm listening."

Triumph gleamed in his expression for an instant as he adjusted his posture, quickly surveyed the room for eavesdroppers. His Adam's apple jumped as he swallowed and leaned closer to me with a hushed whisper.

"Is there somewhere more private we could talk?" he asked.

I kept my arms folded and pulled away from him. His silver eyes reminded me of sunlight sparkling on water. Their self-conscious expression almost charmed me as he clasped his hands uncomfortably behind his back, rocking back and forth on his heels. His change in demeanor seemed odd, causing me to lift an eyebrow at him.

Did he forget he was supposed to be a prince or something?

The similarities between him and my imagined character struck me as unnaturally uncanny.

"No." I stiffened, fear pricking my skin with the suggestion. "You're gonna tell me here or not at all."

He sighed, glancing at Rita who smirked in our direction like Jennica would've if she'd been there. Mischievous and all-too-willing to stay away at the sight of me with a guy.

"Alright . . . Where do I begin?" he muttered to himself, glancing at his feet with nervous laughter.

I tilted my head at him, challenging him to impress me.

"How about why you're here? What made you come looking for me?" I pressed. "How you got here?"

His eyes met mine and he bit his lower lip, clearly trying to come up with the right words.

"Well . . ." He hesitated. "I noticed a change in my dragon form last night. My scales looked different and the need to breathe fire intensified."

When my last words written popped into my thoughts, I cringed. If only he knew how much worse it got.

Snap out of it, Ellie. He's not really—

"Hunters chased me farther into the forest than I've ever gone before. I found a wall of pine trees with a fallen aspen wedged between two of them. When I came to the other side of the wall of trees, I came out looking like this." He indicated to his dark jeans and black T-shirt, tugging on his collar a bit. It gave me another opportunity to take him in without seeming too weird. "My cousin told me once about a Great Writer that he thought might be able to help me break the curse. I'd searched in Tyral, but couldn't find anyone who even closely resembled his description, so when I encountered the magic that changed my appearance, I thought this would be the place to look. A bookstore seemed the most helpful resource for finding information."

If he'd made this up for Mikey's sake, he didn't follow the usual pattern of his other puppets. Most people who were set up to mock me made a little more of a spectacle of it. Mikey always did like making me the brunt of his jokes, especially in public.

"I noticed you while searching the admittedly meager selection in nonfiction for history on magic," he continued, his lip curling slightly as he turned back to the nonfiction section. I followed his gaze only a second. "When I saw how closely the cover of your notebook resembled the Tyral flag, I dropped my book. I've never been so nervous approaching a girl before."

Folding my arms, I leered suspiciously at him, my curiosity rising with every passing second.

"I see. . ." I muttered, taking in everything he said as best I could.

I'd never written anything about a Great Writer. If he really was Prince Erick McKinley, where was this plot twist coming from? Where was he in the story?

"So, this is the first time it's been painful? To change from man to dragon, I mean," I asked, trying to seem casual as I shifted uncomfortably away from the tingling sensation tickling across my skin.

He shifted too, pressing his hands into his pockets awkwardly as if the gesture was foreign and he couldn't relax. "Well, n—no, actually. The first time was last week. This was the first time I noticed a change in my scales."

The seriousness in his voice when he said that seemed so real and matter-of-fact.

"What do your scales look like now as opposed to before?"

"They used to be purely silver. Last night, however, I noticed they had hints of red."

So he's getting close.

"What's the change like?"

If this is a prank, maybe I can at least get some inspiration out of this guy if nothing else.

He hesitated. "Painful? I used to actually enjoy being a dragon. It was freeing and worth the brief pain of transforming to get the feeling of flying."

I blinked, surprised by his attention to detail.

"Even as a human, I've felt more alive and happier. In the last week, especially, I've felt more . . . angry. Even over completely stupid things."

My mind wandered to my own words.

His blood boiled with a level of fury he didn't recognize as he resisted the urge to grab the throat of the guard. Even his voice seemed different as he ordered the man to get his father.

His breath tasted like smoke, ashes tingling on the tip of his tongue with a gritty sensation that exhilarated him like never before.

He was powerful. And he wanted more.

My heart sunk. "Really?" I asked, hoping he'd change the story he told.

Instead, he nodded, rubbing the back of his neck again. Something Erick McKinley did when he felt nervous. "It scares me. When I confided in my cousin, he told me to stay as far into the woods as I could when I change from now on."

I hesitated, trying to piece all of this together in a sensical way without throwing myself into believing him wholeheartedly.

"S—so, how'd you get here?" I asked, my voice cracking slightly.

"I said I've been searching everywhere for you," he began after a silence. "I meant that. I'd heard legends about you, but never knew where to look. Sorcerers and magic have been sparse since I was cursed. So, looking for you in Tyral didn't make—"

"Tyral?" I tested, lifting my eyebrows challengingly.

He chuckled lightly, his mannerisms becoming a little more relaxed as he leaned against a shelf the shape of a large book and folded his arms. "My kingdom. You'd love it, I'm sure." He winked playfully. "It's a really beautiful place."

I couldn't help but smile as I resisted the overpowering need to giggle like a fangirl. My imagination drew up vivid descriptions of everything. The castle's steeples and towers stretching into a bright blue, cloudless sky. A stone wall surrounding the village, encompassed by forest. A large field of wildflowers. I imagined Erick grazing his fingers across the tall grass as he headed home after a change.

My focus wandered toward him and, for the first time, I had a face to put to my character. A physical person to fit his description in my head.

Hearing him speak so casually about his—*my*—kingdom sent shivers of excitement through my system. I bit down on my growing smile as I tried to refrain from giving away how excited I really felt.

"It's real?" I squeaked, hearing everyone from Mom to Jennica and Mikey telling me how much other people didn't care about my story and I needed to keep myself under control.

"No one wants to hear about that, Ellie. Maybe you should just mellow out a little."

I sniffed, mirroring his position and flipping my hair casually. "I mean . . . it's *real?"*

I couldn't hold back my giddiness anymore and it burst through in a high-pitched giggle that surprised even me. Self-conscious, I covered my mouth to restrain myself.

It didn't help.

Laughing, he watched me with lifted eyebrows and an amused grin.

"Of course it's real."

I sighed, feeling weak at the knees as I pressed my back against the bookshelf and slid to the floor, covering my mouth with the shock of conflicting emotions flustering inside me like a flock of butterflies.

He knelt beside me, gently tucking two fingers below my chin and guiding my focus to look at him. I didn't even care, though feeling his touch made me shiver with exhilaration.

He seemed so real and believable. I felt like I'd been pulled into a vortex of hazy words. I knew his voice so well. The world seemed to blur behind him in a surreal haze swirling around me like a vortex of words and daydreams.

"Will you help me?" he asked, his voice hesitant yet hopeful.

"Will I—help . . ." My voice a bubbly hum in my throat, I gazed into those misty eyes. I lost myself in the illusion of him. His presence felt suddenly like nothing more than a mirage. An ethereal entity. Completely unbelievable, but real nonetheless.

He was close. Too close.

His presence pestered me and I felt enthralled in the way he looked into me like he saw everything I felt, every beat of my pounding heart.

Beneath his intense stare, I felt vulnerable and somehow important. Unworthy of the pedestal he'd placed me on, yet capable of moving mountains.

I had no *real* power. I wasn't a sorcerer or anything like that. I couldn't help him. But the way he seemed to believe I was something so grand was intoxicating. I wanted to be that for him. I'd always wished I could do something so important. Be a hero rather than an omniscient storyteller. I wanted to save him from the corner I'd written him into with that curse. I glanced at my notebook, thinking of the words and scene I'd just written and my daze quickly shifted into fear.

If he told the truth . . . Did I just kill him?

"Come with me, Ellie," he purred quietly. "I promise I won't hurt you."

Chapter 4

"Was it all a dream?"

~ Ellie's Story

Looking into his eyes, I saw a piece of me reflected in him. I knew him intimately, though I'd never seen him a day in my life. I knew everything about the character he professed to be. I knew how dangerous he could be, both emotionally and physically. He'd destroy me if he were real. It would only get worse.

I had to be dreaming. Perhaps I'd fallen asleep while writing and I'd wake up with paper stuck to my cheek.

His words whirled in my thoughts again and again. I knew it wouldn't end well for him. But something in the way he looked at me reeked of sincerity. He meant those words. He wouldn't *want* to hurt me. But in his dragon form, would he really have a choice?

Dream or not, the possibility of seeing the kingdom I'd heard and written about for eighteen years excited me. Jennica told me I needed more adventure in my life, though I didn't yearn for the kind of adventures she referred to.

Maybe I really am too timid.

"Come on," he said, standing with a hand offered to help me up. "Come with me, Ellie." He spoke slowly, his gentle tone thick with the temptation to do his bidding. Just the right amount of authority to make me want to obey.

I stared at his hand, his fingers wiggling a bit to invite me to take it. The idea of touching him again froze my body in place. The urge became powerful enough to help me refrain as I stood, folded my arms, and stepped away from him.

A question in his eyes told me he hadn't expected my reaction.

"L—lead the way," I said warily, pointing toward the door, but keeping my arms folded in rejection of his offered hand.

His brow creased and he stood straighter. "Why didn't you—"

"Let's go." I walked toward the door, hugging my torso firmly. The rain left only a few trickles plopping into the puddles at my feet.

The door shut behind me and hit his shoulder as he followed me outside.

"Wait," he called, rushing to my side.

I sauntered quickly toward the canopy of trees surrounding my hometown like a wall. Something told me to keep moving and not look back. Something pushed me forward . . . away from his physical presence. I couldn't handle it right then. My body felt cold with memories I couldn't quite understand. They were nothing but a jumbled mess in my thoughts. Trying to piece them together made my heart pound uncomfortably in my throat.

I only remembered how many times I'd been hurt by the hands of a guy. How stupid it was that I couldn't even look at them without feeling anxiety fluster in my stomach. Being touched by Erick sent fiery shocks through my nerves. My skin seemed to remember what it felt like to be squeezed so tightly that fingerprints indented my forearms. His knuckles turning white from the strength of his unwavering grip. The goosebumps forming pricked my skin with painful memories.

I didn't stop walking until he caught up to me beneath the shelter of leaves and branches overhead.

"I'm sorry, is taking a man's hand not proper here?" he asked when he caught up to me.

Embarrassed, I glanced at the hand he casually hid in his jean's pocket and my chin tingled where those fingers had touched me. Subconsciously, I touched the spot, if only to assure myself that I'd been the last person to touch my skin. My spine tingled with regret and an uncontrollable urge to stay as far from those hands as I could.

"It's . . . different from what I'm used to, that's all," I muttered in weak response.

His lips pressed firmly together with a look of confusion that struck me as almost cute.

"Why?"

I sighed, scrambling to think of an excuse. "Most guys I know just don't even think of helping a girl stand like that. I'm not used to it."

Now please stop pressing me about it.

He brushed a finger across his nose, crossing his arms behind his back. "This place is so strange," he muttered to himself, walking in a pose I'd only seen men in classic movies like *Pride and Prejudice* or *Jane Eyre* use. "What other customs are you not used to?"

A laugh burst free at the timing of that question.

"Well, most guys don't walk like Mr. Darcy," I scoffed, gesturing to him.

He narrowed his eyes at me. "Who's Mr. Darcy?"

I hesitated, unsure how to respond. "Umm, he's . . . Nobody."

"You're more in love with a stupid fictional character than you are with me."

That memory of Mikey's words made me shudder and I prayed he wouldn't press me to continue.

Head held high, he walked with a princely poise I would've expected from my character.

"Alright." He shrugged, holding a branch of thick leaves out of my way and letting me go ahead of him. "What do you do when you're not writing?"

I spat an exasperated sound disguised as a laugh. Writing was the most exciting thing about my life.

"School, mostly. And venturing into well-known forests with complete strangers who claim to be my characters. You know, totally normal stuff."

He laughed, a loud and awkward sound that made me want to return the favor.

"So, this is what you might consider normal then?"

I nodded playfully, enjoying light-hearted conversation. "Oh, yeah. Tomorrow, I'll probably meet someone new who will whisk me away to some fairytale land."

His laughter diminished some as we ducked around trees and branches. "I see, so you're *that* kind of girl," he teased, glancing at me from the corner of his eye with a sly lift of his brow.

I looked at him, surprised by his assumption of my character, and opened my mouth to respond but too shocked to come up with much.

Scoffing again, I broke eye contact and watched our feet move together, thinking of all the times Jennica tried convincing me to hook up with random guys she considered attractive. She saw dating as a game while I took dating seriously, which was why I often neglected the subject of romance outside of a writer's standpoint. After Mikey, I only added it to stories out of obligation to future readers.

"Yeah, I'm definitely the kind of girl who runs off with just anyone," I mumbled sarcastically, brushing my fingers across the needles of a nearby pine tree.

He chuckled, something changing in his countenance. Mischievous and playful, but mysterious and dangerous. Instantly, I regretted the comment.

"No, I'm really not," I back-pedaled, hoping he really didn't think I was that easily persuaded. "I'm about as far away from promiscuous, or even adventurous, as you can get without being considered a nun."

He hesitated after that, though he watched me with a sort of enchantment in his eye that would've made my knees weak if I'd looked at him directly.

"We'll see about that." His smirk a bit cocky, he turned his attention forward again, relieving me of his gaze. His words made me uncomfortable. I wasn't a project to be used for experiments on how far he could get me to go.

"What does that mean?" A twig cracked beneath my foot, snapping the otherwise silent air in half. He smirked, amused.

I bit my lip as embarrassment made its way into my cheeks. He didn't even seem to notice that he stared at me. He seemed completely lost in thought. Like he didn't realize he watched someone until they felt completely uneasy. I'd done that enough times to know the feeling. People watching was one of my favorite hobbies, though it often backfired on me when I got yelled at for staring too long at someone.

"So, I'm assuming you know these forests pretty intimately."

Uneasy, I narrowed my eyes at his avoidance. However, I couldn't help but smile at the memories that flashed in my head as I breathed in the crisp, fresh air of early autumn. I remembered Dad and me jumping into piles of leaves and pine needles. I remembered the sharp pricking of leaves on my skin as I shuffled around them. Laughing with him as he hoisted me into the air, tossing me up and down. I remembered him holding me high and running around, pretending to turn me into a dragon so I could "fly."

It was the most fun I'd ever had.

"My dad and I explored this forest together for most of my childhood. He taught me how to love creating things, especially stories. He made that notebook for me, actually."

"He was an artist then?"

I laughed at the understatement. "I guess you could say that. Although, I'd call him more of a creator since he could make something wonderful from nothing no matter the medium. There were so many different ideas he'd come up with. It seemed like he always had an endless plethora of them. He was my best friend before. . ." I trailed off, my voice cut off by emotion before I could finish the sentence.

The last memory I had of him was in that forest. He warned me not to wander, blowing me a kiss before turning his back and walking away. I assumed he headed back home, but never saw him again.

Erick waited for me to continue before flashing an inquisitive look my way. I forced my gaze downward in avoidance.

"Before . . ." he urged, leaning forward to see my expression. I turned away.

"Nothing," I muttered, biting back the tears threatening to manifest themselves.

"You're not very good at hiding your feelings." His tone caressed my fears in a soothing and teasing manner. That only made the urge to cry stronger. "Did something happen to him?"

I glared at the ground, not used to anyone seeing right through me. Suddenly, his questions seemed way too personal. Too probing. Flashes of irrational anger spat at me, tempting me to shrivel and throw it at him.

"I told you, it's nothing," I snapped, startled by the intensity of my own reaction.

The slightest shift in his expression implied he didn't believe me. He didn't continue, remaining silent for a while. His gaze, however, stuck to me like glue. He only looked away to hold a branch over my head so I could pass ahead of him a few times.

Any time a guy looked at me like that before, I'd felt incredibly uncomfortable, wanting to hide from the shame it brought. But with him, it seemed different. Almost welcomed. He didn't seem to look at me like a hawk honing in on a mouse. He looked at me with meaning and depth. I couldn't have been *that* fascinating to look at, yet his scrutiny was fixed and curious.

I swallowed nerves bubbling into my throat and ducked around branches. If he kept this up, I'd turn back and pray he didn't follow me.

"You know, you're much prettier than I would've imagined," he observed thoughtfully.

Caught off-guard, I snapped to attention and stiffened, rubbing the goosebumps on my arms. My eyes scanned the forest to find a physical place to hide as my legs carried me forward. If I'd known that's what he thought of, I never would've gone.

What had I just walked into?

I felt danger creeping into my body, though nothing about his demeanor implied it. He seemed genuinely fascinated by me. When he looked at me, he didn't seem to notice my figure like Mikey always did. It was almost like he saw straight into my soul. Like he saw everything. Not only the outer shell, but my core. With one look, I felt helpless to resist believing him when he said I was pretty.

I couldn't speak. If I could've, I wouldn't have known what to say. I could only hope that avoiding eye contact would also help me avoid his power over me. I wouldn't give that to him. I couldn't give him the opportunity.

"Wow, you're right," he remarked, breaking his concentration to look downward.

"What am I right about?" I asked cautiously, hoping I didn't look too dumb for not listening if he'd been talking.

"You really are as solitary as a nun. Most women would've swooned at that."

He was testing me?

A flash of anger erupted inside of me for an instant before I let out a bellowing laugh in spite of myself.

That's definitely something Erick would do.

"You're quite a player, aren't you?" I teased, unsettled by memories of my own writing.

The beauty in her eyes was hard to look away from, shining a shade of blue as dazzling as the night sky.

How long would it take for her to fall in love with him?

I sighed, regretting those words immensely. I'd made him so on purpose because I never thought I'd ever face that in person.

He chuckled low in his throat, a sound that gave me pause at how familiar and oddly comforting it felt to me.

"Player, huh?" His air of confidence beamed with the smirk on his face. "That's a new one. What else you think of me."

I sighed, regretting now that I'd written a character with every quality my heart feared most. Before Mikey, it hadn't bothered me.

Now, however . . .

"Nice try," I retorted, feigning annoyance by rolling my eyes.

"Come on, Ellie," he chortled, dodging a tree branch again. "You can't hide it from me for long."

"If you try anything with me, that's a good way to get a knee to the groin," I warned, my tone teasing, but my intent serious. I couldn't afford any more heartache.

His eyes softened with a tilt of his head. He walked backward so he could look at me again.

"Duly noted. Can't blame me for trying." He winked at me.

I frowned.

I didn't want him to try.

When I looked up and realized where we stood, I halted. I knew that clearing. I knew every tiny detail. It wasn't far from my backyard. A dense wall of evergreens surrounded the untouched, fallen tree breaking through with a peek of what lie beyond. It'd been there as long as I could remember.

I hadn't seen it since the day he left us. Since the day he left *me.*

Chapter 5

"The scales of a dragon determine if they're trustworthy. His stained red as blood."

~ Ellie's Story

Breath caught in my throat, nearly choking me. Memories flooded into my consciousness, so numerous and vivid I couldn't concentrate. Every one of them revolved around times I'd shared with Dad.

I saw us playing on the ground the day he told me about a kingdom deep within the forest.

My inspiration for Tyral.

I saw him showing me a magic trick when he told me about the sorcerers in that world.

That's what made my story a fantasy.

I heard him growling as he chased me around the trees playing hide and seek, pretending to be the dragon of legends.

My inspiration for . . .

"Ellie?"

I flinched right before the last memory plagued my thoughts.

I saw myself standing on the fallen tree, looking out at the world beyond as a fifteen-year-old girl. I yearned to know what hid behind the mysterious wall of trees. To know if something really was back there worth seeing or if it was nothing more than trees and bushes and ferns.

My focus wandered past the fallen tree, haunted by the sound of Dad's screams as he ordered me to never go back there alone. How I could've gotten hurt and he wouldn't have been there to protect me.

I scoffed at that memory. He ended up being more right about that one than I ever thought at the time.

Goosebumps tingled across my arms with a shiver as I stumbled backward.

My dazed focus finally landed on Erick, his expression concerned and confused.

"What's wrong?" he asked, reaching out to stabilize me.

Something shifted in me, a sense of nostalgia creeping in. I said nothing, furrowing my brow and approaching the large tree. Dreamily, my fingers brushed across the tree's rough and beloved texture.

"Don't you ever go near this tree alone again, Ellie, do you understand me? Quit playing around back here or you're going to hurt yourself."

I cringed and pulled my hand toward my chest when my eyes found the engraving Dad etched into the trunk. *Daddy's Little Girl,* with a heart around it. Emotion tugged on my throat and made it hard to swallow.

"I haven't been here in so long," I whispered, mostly to myself.

"Why?" Erick asked, leaning against the engraving.

Part of me wanted him to scoot away as if sitting on it would somehow ruin it.

The sincerity in his countenance urged me to trust him. To open up and not be afraid of his ridicule. Something in me knew he would understand like no one else would.

Swallowing my pride, I let a light smile brush my lips as I stroked the tree.

"Dad used to tell me stories about a kingdom with dragons, and sorcerers, and magic. They were his favorite stories to tell. He used to tell me about the prince who lived in a castle and a dragon that flew in the sky at night that no one could ever catch. I spent a lot of time here with him as a kid, up until about five years ago when he disappeared."

My words caught on that last word. *Disappeared.* He was gone. The idea left me feeling numb with sorrow and longing for the daddy I'd never truly know.

I swallowed past the lump and continued.

"He told me to stay away from this tree. He told me there was a reason, but never told me. Only 'I'll tell you when you're older.' You know, the thing parents say to their kids when they really don't want to talk about something?"

Erick chuckled, nodding with a gentle smirk.

I continued. "Yeah, he promised to show me someday, but disappeared before he could. Sometimes I wonder if he left just so he wouldn't ever have to tell me."

An unexpected spike of anger flared inside me. Immediately, I pushed it away with an insincere laugh and watched a pinecone I kicked back and forth.

I noticed Erick's expression change slightly to curiosity, but ignored the question in his fixed gaze.

"He told me stories about everything because, to him, stories *were* everything. He had the wildest imagination of anyone I've ever met. Guess that's where I get it from. I always did take after my daddy."

I smiled, touching my blonde hair and remembering what his felt like.

"The last memory I have of him was with this tree. He never wanted me to wander to the other side. I assumed he didn't want me wandering off to where he couldn't keep track of me. Now. . ." I hesitated, stroking the scratchy bark as emotion tightened my throat. "I'll never know."

Telling someone who didn't already know him left me with a gaping hole in my chest, raw and vulnerable beneath Erick's magnifying glass stare. I hardly noticed the words dancing off my lips until after I'd said them. The relief surprised me. I hadn't realized how much I'd held inside.

Not many people would indulge me anymore with talking about him. My family certainly wouldn't have listened. Brock and Jennica had gotten sick of hearing the same stories again and again. The simple act of voicing those memories released them into the air and pulled some of their pain out of me.

"I used to spend a lot of time writing here. Something about it fascinated me. He left me that day, warning me to stay on the safe side. He blew me a kiss before heading back home. At least, I *thought* he went back home. A few hours later, my sister came asking me if I'd seen Dad. She was so worried. We searched for him everywhere, but couldn't find him. We went to the police and they passed it off as abandonment after a week of searching. I haven't seen him since."

Erick's attention seemed completely engulfed by me. I blushed under his soft and compassionate gaze. I'd shared way more than I ever intended.

"This is probably too personal to be telling you," I muttered, coyly tucking my hair behind my ear. I'd never opened up so much to a guy so soon after meeting them. Yet it felt as natural as talking to a lifelong friend.

"No, please," he said, pushing himself away from the tree. "Continue. I like listening to you."

Somber, I scrutinized him in search of sincerity. His silver eyes glinted with a calm and reassuring smile that created small crinkles around them. He was sincere . . . at least in his smile.

"You have a way with words that captivates me," he said slowly, seeming dazed.

The compliment swelled inside me, filling me with warmth and pride. I sighed, folding my arms protectively around me to keep that feeling from shining through.

"Yeah, sure," I muttered, brushing my fingers across a nearby fern to avoid his fixed gaze.

"You don't believe me?"

A feeble laugh escaped from me like a cough. I didn't want to believe him, but he spoke so earnestly. His intent was to persuade me to help him, after all. If he had to sweet-talk his way to victory, he would.

Meandering around the clearing, I watched the tip of my shoe kick leaves and dirt around the forest floor. I felt relaxed being there after the initial shock wore off. The peace surrounding the area seemed too sacred to disturb with noise. That was why I liked it there so much. Natural beauty reminded me of better times, pulling me in with its honey-sweet song of the wind in trees and water rolling over rocks in the stream.

"So, where's my kingdom, Prince Erick? All I've seen is the forest. I see that every day." I nodded toward the trees around us.

He chuckled, interrupted by a sharp gasp as he twisted his neck and moaned. Something shimmered on his cheek, just under his sideburn.

I squinted and wondered if I'd imagined the subtle detail.

"Maybe this will help," he muttered, hoisting himself onto the fallen tree wedged between two pines. Walking along its trunk like a tightrope, he turned and grinned slyly at me before hopping off on the other side.

"No," I shouted, instinctively reaching for him.

Thick lavender smoke sprang from the ground at his feet, quickly enveloping him until it consumed his entire body. When it dissipated as fast as it'd come, he wore a black tailcoat, knickers, and leather boots to the knees. The silver crown on his head glittered with amethyst, diamonds, and sapphires.

I blinked, my jaw dropped as he approached me.

Whatever I expected, I hadn't expected that.

"H—how did you . . ." My eyes scanned his appearance over and over again.

I never thought a guy dressed in Victorian garb would be so . . . appealing.

Involuntarily, words weaved into my subconscious and my fingers ached to write them down.

He tugged on the ruffles of the tunic sleeves, leaning against the tree with a wicked grin.

Stunned, I watched him approach the fallen tree. He chuckled, grinning triumphantly as he bowed like a magician finishing an elaborate trick before leaning against the fallen tree.

A shudder rolled over me. The frilly silk of his cravat glimmered with amethysts sewn into the hem as it ruffled over his chest and tucked into his waistcoat.

I drew a deep breath, trying to absorb what happened.

"I dare you to not believe me now," he teased, his crooked smile smug as he plucked off a piece of bark and twirled it between his fingers.

Something in his voice gave me goosebumps. Suddenly, I saw nothing but Prince Erick Julien McKinley.

"How'd you do that?"

I thought Dad's magic tricks were impressive. This made those seem like child's play.

Is that what would've happened if I'd crossed over before? Would it happen now?

The clouded light reflected the pride in Erick's eyes when he laughed, making them sparkle. Scales shimmered across his skin, slowly becoming more noticeable as they crawled across either side of his neck. I swallowed, walking to the tree again.

"I told you. I'm your character. Magic like this is normal to me." Mischief tinted his smile inching along his face as he whispered, "Come with me, Ellie."

I tentatively sat on the engraving Dad made. "I'm good."

"Come on," he urged, picking up my hand and tugging gently. Yanking it back, I folded my arms and shot him a dark glare in silent warning.

He watched me in confusion for only a second before nodding. "Right. Sorry."

"Nothing good will come from this. I'm not going."

His gentle smile reassured and frightened me at the same time.

"Ellie." He offered me his hand again, palm up and inviting. "Just trust me."

I stared at it, my breath quickening as my eyes darted between his hand and face.

If I take that hand, there's no way of knowing where he'll take me.

I shook my head in disbelief.

My character is offering me his hand. I could see my kingdom. The place I've dreamed about since I was a kid.

What're you waiting for, Ellie?

If I took his hand and let him lead me into what lie beyond familiar, it would mean I'd be plunging face-first into something I wasn't sure I wanted any part of.

People would die because of him . . . because of *me.* If that were going to happen, did I really want to be witness to it? My gaze found the scales glistening on his cheeks.

Silver. Only a tiny bit of red.

He should safe for a little while . . . As safe as a dragon could be.

If I went with him, I'd face the reality of choices I'd made during creative stupors where words controlled me. I'd face the reality of the mistakes I'd made and the lives I'd put in danger with my pen on paper.

If I didn't go, however, I'd never know what might've been.

Memories of my story flashed in my mind with feelings of guilt and fear.

Maybe it was best I didn't go.

"Ellie, my arm's getting tired," he remarked, a lighthearted smile in his tone. "I'm not going to hurt you."

"Somehow, I doubt that," I sighed, annoyed at the intoxicating temptation to trust him.

He was anything but safe for me.

"It's the only way to move forward, Ellie."

I frowned. Going beyond that tree also meant deliberately disobeying one of the last wishes Dad gave me. But did I really want to spend the rest of my life wondering what it would've been like to step into fantasy? And if I got into a habit of taking his hand, what kind of threshold would that cross?

Why are you so scared, Ellie? You'll never find an opportunity like this again.

I sighed again, trying to piece together how I felt.

I'm not taking that hand. I know he'll rope me into his trap if I do.

Take it, Ellie. You know you want to.

I can't finish anything I start with him.

Maybe you will. Maybe there's a way you can change the outcome for him. You'll never know if you don't take that hand.

I hated my emotions for their power over me.

Timidly, I unfolded my arms and rested my fingers on his upturned palm. I tried ignoring the exhilarating thrill I got from the warmth of his hand. His smile broadened as he slowly tugged me onto the tree. I swallowed nervously walking across it. My heart pounded and I cringed, hearing Dad yelling at me to stay away from there.

You never told me why.

A thrill shivered up my spine with the sense of dishonesty and betrayal I felt in deliberately disobeying him.

Erick's fingers held tighter as he helped me jump off. I scolded my heart for thumping against my chest.

As soon as my feet landed on the unknown turf, I felt something nipping the tips of my toes. The sensation rushed through my body quickly like I'd stood up too fast. Lavender smoke clouded my vision, smelling like flowers and tasting like candy.

Blinking away the shocking illusion, I looked down to see my jeans and T-shirt replaced with light blue skirts draped from my hips. Layers of petticoats brushed my legs under the silky skirts and swayed when I moved.

My head reeled, the world around me hazy. White, lace gloves decorated my arms. I gasped, though my breath cut short. I ran my hands down my stomach, stiff with a corset. The bodice adorned my torso with the same fine lace as the gloves, but with rhinestones and embroidered roses throughout. The broad neckline wrapped around my upper arms, leaving my neck area exposed.

Feeling my hair on my bare shoulders sent an exhilarating thrill down my back. My lungs constricted, left unsatisfied.

"I don't believe this," I exhaled, far too anxious for more oxygen. I turned to Erick who stared at me with distracted astonishment.

Suddenly, I became aware of exposed skin and tugged at the top of my dress neckline in an effort to cover myself better.

I looked down to see cleavage. Not much, but enough to make me uncomfortable. My cheeks hot, I covered it. His expression made me feel raw and vulnerable, but also gave me an oddly satisfying feeling of being pretty and admired.

"Wow," he finally said.

"What?" Instinctively, I took a step away, tripping on a layer of petticoat.

Erick's lips twitched into a smile for half a second. "I thought of you as something of a deity before, but now. . ."

An involuntary giggle escaped as I bowed my head to hide from his words.

"Now, you see that I'm just a girl in a pretty dress," I said, hoping to dodge the compliment by twirling. I loved the sway of skirts around my legs.

"No." His smile calm, he rested his head against the trunk of a tree, crossing one leg over the other. "You never were *just a girl.* I've just never seen a girl look so . . . miraculous."

"Miraculous?" I might've scoffed at the word choice if I hadn't been too busy giggling like an idiot. My fingers grazed the light fabric again. I certainly *felt* miraculous in that gown and I wanted to bask in that feeling a while. I hadn't felt so beautiful since the party Mikey threw for my last birthday.

The memory pricked my skin like a bee sting. Instinctively, I shooed it away and forced myself to be numb again.

Why? Don't be numb now. You're in a gown, for Heaven's sake! Enjoy it.

I picked up the light blue overlay and spun around, letting the fabric flow behind me. I sighed and giggled and spun, feeling free of any care in the world. Until the heel of my boot caught on the petticoat and I stumbled.

Erick caught me in an instant, holding me against him. The world still spun while my focus cleared and I found his eyes smiling down at me.

Dazed, I stared into his startling, crimson eyes, mesmerized by the shimmering scales rippling across his irises. His features shaded in the dim light of a sun hiding behind the horizon.

My breath caught up with the rapid speed of my heart pounding against my ribcage. All the places he touched tingled with intensity and fiery warning. Sensations circulated in frenzied panic as I stood straight, tossing him away from me. My fingers grazed my waist, head, hands, trying to erase his touch from my skin's memory. It did nothing, but only exaggerated the tingling areas of my waist where his fingers had gripped me to hold me steady. Wiping my hands on silky skirts only reminded me of how warm and inviting his hand felt in mine.

Stop it, Ellie, I scolded internally, awkwardly handling my hair.

Erick stared at me, confusion in his skeptical brow. "You're certainly jumpy. What's—"

His eyes grew distant as he gazed into a sky fading into night. His shoulders slumped with abrupt exhaustion, eyes dazed as his consciousness waned.

I backed away, recognizing his symptoms instantly. I didn't want to be close to him if he shape-shifted into a dragon.

Slight moonlight seeped through the canopy of leaves, illuminating part of his face in the low twilight. His head fell limply to the side before he winced, the muscles in his neck tightening.

He lurched forward, gripping his sides as the scales I'd noticed before quickly slithered across his hairline and cheeks. He inhaled, a grunt cutting his breath short like he'd been punched in the stomach. Shaking, he fell to his knees and moaned in pain.

The change had begun.

Chapter 6

"Never did he feel freer than when he could let go and just fly."

~ Ellie's Story

Erick," I shrieked, not caring about how hard I hit the forest floor. At least the layers of petticoats helped break my fall. His hair hung forward, covering his face from view. He prodded his sides, holding himself tightly around the torso and moaning.

Help him, dope.

His body convulsed, eyes squeezed shut as scales distorted his hands and neck. His choppy breath sliced through the air in puffs of smoke that reeked like freshly doused fire. The sound he made was unnatural and nearly inhuman.

He reeled as bones and muscles shifted inside him. His fingernails grew into long, sharp talons. His lips pulled back, revealing radiant fangs. Breath hissed from between them in sharp gasps.

"Get back, Ellie," he growled, his hair dangling over his warning eyes as he glared at me. Scales nearly completely encompassed his face.

"Holy *crap.*" I didn't even care that the branches speckling the ground cut my hands as I tumbled away from him. I couldn't get away fast enough. The pain barely phased me when the back of my head whacked into the rough texture of the fallen tree.

The same lavender smoke that'd surrounded him before swirled into the air. When it dissipated, a dragon stood, neck extended into the trees. Dim light reflected off each silvery scale like mirrors.

The creature shook its head as if waking from a nap. I heard its thick pant from where I sat, cowering, on the ground. Breath stilled as I whipped my head around when the claws of a briar patch pricked my head and neck. I tried scrambling further into hiding, but only slipped on the leaves covering the ground like a blanket of snow.

The dragon turned toward me, piercing red eyes staring straight at me. Just like the dragon imprinted on my notebook.

So much for hiding.

Bat-like wings hugged the sides of its body. Frill connected the spikes and horns on its head like webbing. Its tail whipped behind its enormous figure, eventually wrapping around its hind legs like a cat. At the tip, frill extended like the fan of a mermaid's tail. Burgundy spikes flared out from its jawline and down its back.

It set its feet down on the forest floor, gradually approaching me.

My mind scrambled and I would've screamed if my throat and mouth hadn't dried to the point it hurt to swallow. I would've run if I'd had anywhere to go. Trees surrounded us with unfamiliar and suddenly dangerous mystery.

Frantically, I searched my surroundings for a better place to hide. I didn't know how conscious he was of his human self while in that form. If he had even the slightest bit of red dragon in him, his consciousness of humanity would dwindle.

Nowhere to go. It had me cornered. Trapped.

The bulky dress I wore hindered my agility. I cursed the silky fabric catching on every rock and twig below me.

The dragon towered over me, a low purr rumbling in its throat as it approached and leaned closer.

I blinked, surprised by the gentle nature of the beast.

The sound brought me back to when Pepper lay on my stomach, curled into a contented ball of fur. Heat resonated from its massive form. It looked me directly in the eyes. Silver lined the pupils, slashing through the scarlet shade, glistening with the same, scale-like effect I'd seen before.

"E—Erick?"

In a moment of blind courage, I extended my hand toward it.

Releasing another purr, the beast nuzzled its snout the size of my torso against my palm. Laughter choked in my throat with disbelief.

Its scales felt strange. Warm and soft, yet coarse and ridged. Deep red colored the root of each scale, fading into a gradient of silver as bright as the moon.

His curse is getting stronger.

He was changing from a fun-loving, mischievous silver dragon into an anger-driven, aggressive red dragon. I wondered how much time he had before the curse made its final shift.

Dread blackened my soul a bit with that observation.

His only hope was an honest confession of love.

Instantly, my thoughts turned to how he'd looked at *me* when I'd first crossed over the fallen tree. The compliments he'd given me earlier.

Panic rushed through my blood, making me feel hot and anxious.

No way is he using me as a means of breaking his curse.

The dragon's eyes held my gaze. I knew those eyes. Resting my other hand below its jaw, I ran my fingers along the bridge of its snout.

But are you really going to let him die just to protect yourself?

The dragon chuffed like a tiger, stepping away with a playful spring in its step.

It was cute how excited he seemed, drastically different from the human Erick I'd seen writhing in pain. This was typical behavior of his dragon form, though still unsettling after having just witnessed his transformation.

Couldn't I just let him fall in love with me and I stay platonic? That wouldn't hurt anyone, right?

He circled around me, nudging me playfully with his snout.

"Hey," I laughed, stumbling forward.

He tossed his head, eyes twinkling with fun. I smiled, shaking my head at his charming demeanor.

Yes. That would hurt everyone. You can't break his curse and remain platonic.

I stroked his nose again, the edges of each scale scraping against my fingertips.

It felt so . . . *real.*

A giddy tickle in my throat brought with it a realization that it was real. *He* was real.

I let loose a hesitant laugh in my deep exhale and rolled my fingers over the rough horns lining the bridge of his snout. Erick pulled away, turning around the trees, flipping his tail as he weaved through them like playing hide-and-seek. With an amused smile, I shook my head. Eyes glittering with mischief when he chuffed again, flipping his head toward his back.

"What?"

A deep growl filled the air as he glared. He flipped his head again, pointing his snout toward his back.

He wants me to get on his back? He must think I'm crazy.

Exhaling in a gust, I stared at his back.

Maybe I really am crazy.

I could only prove it by getting on his back and let him take me away in flight.

I could go flying on the back of my dragon.

An unexpected burst of excitement shivered through me and I bit back a giddy smile. Every fantasy writer dreamed of this moment.

I could've argued logically for hours about how irrational and idiotic the decision was, but that certainly didn't stop me from climbing awkwardly onto the back of the dragon while muttering, "I can't believe I'm doing this."

I closed my eyes and straddled his back as best I could, gripping his neck tightly. Erick growled at me and shook my hold loose.

"Sorry," I said, realizing that my fingernails dug at a patch of his scales. "I didn't mean to."

What on earth are you doing, Ellie? You're gonna die doing this. They'll have to write on your tombstone that you died on the back of a dragon.

The thought made me hesitate.

Maybe that wouldn't be such a bad way to go. . .

Shaking my head of that thought process, I gripped onto one of the horns lining Erick's back.

"Be gentle, please," I whined, fear trembling through me with an early wave of motion sickness.

He turned his head around to look at me, a playful smirk in his eyes. His large wings extended wide, fanning out to expose just how grand they really were. When I looked back and saw his silvery, translucent wings stretched out to their full capacity, I gasped in awe. Moonlight reflecting off them made their thin texture glow. He looked back at his wings and proudly puffed out his chest a bit.

I turned back to him and laughed. "Showoff."

He chuffed and took a couple of long strides forward before launching himself off the ground.

A scream ripped through my throat and I grabbed his neck again, holding on for my life.

My stomach got left behind as the beat of Erick's mighty wings carried us farther into the atmosphere. My hair whipped against the air, stinging as it slapped my cheeks. I gasped as the wind got knocked out of me, burying my face in Erick's scaly neck to breathe again.

This is it. This is how I'm going to die. Riding a reckless dragon.

Another growl thundered in Erick's chest.

Startled, I sat up and instantly found the ground farther away than before. Trees and houses looked like pieces of a patchwork quilt. The wave of nausea I swallowed burned my esophagus as it glided back down. I shuddered, my heart pounding in my ears so loudly it nearly drowned out the sound of Erick's wings.

At least we were stationary and not flying any higher. I looked out at the black night and breathed slowly, afraid of disturbing the air around me. Numberless stars glittered in galaxies, twisting and swirling around us with wisps of light. I'd never felt so small yet so important.

Erick glided forward gently, apparently satisfied by my contented sigh.

Cold air weaved through my hair and ruffled my skirts. I tried absorbing every detail of how I felt in that moment. I wanted to remember how the mist felt on my tongue as we rode the clouds. The rough texture of Erick's scales under my fingers. The clear air as crisp and delicious as the freedom I experienced. The world I knew seemed miles away. Any cares I had before became insignificant as I let my head fall heavenward, reaching out to touch the universe.

Purrs rumbled from Erick's stomach when he glanced my way with a lighthearted gleam in his red eyes.

I could feel my burdens physically lifted with the thin clouds dissipating between my fingers. I laughed. For the first time in what felt like an eternity, my laugh came as easily as breathing.

You shouldn't be happy about this.

I paused, an unexplained feeling of dread sinking into my soul and spreading shadows over joy.

Why shouldn't I? This was everything I'd ever dreamed of. Something every writer dreamed of. Seeing their work jump off the page and spring to life with vigor.

Remember what you've done to him.

All at once, my fingertips grew cold and numb. A burn in my chest chilled with the realization that I'd already written the ending to Erick's story. His curse would only get worse. He wasn't supposed to fall in love in the end. He fell prey to . . .

A sickening feeling seeped through my system, pulling me closer to Erick's warm back. I yearned for the comfort of knowing he was still there. Still alive.

His destiny was in my hands.

What have I done? And how will I fix it?

Chapter 7

"Darkness enshrouded his being, implying danger in every movement."

~ *Ellie's Story*

Dawn bled through my eyelids and I groaned, begrudgingly opening my eyes. Blurry vision made the world foggy. I stirred, my spine sore from leaning against something hard. I sat up, stretching and rubbing my tired eyes as my brain registered where I was.

The surface around me felt like a cloud, light and fluffy. All at once, memories of the night before flooded into me and I sat up, my focus finally adjusting to the extravagant room around me.

I blinked hard, rubbing my eyes again to make sure I wasn't dreaming.

The illusion remained. Every breathtaking detail clear.

A few bronze-colored love seats sat around the room. A large window towered to the high ceiling. Thick, white curtains draped to the ground, bunched to the sides to allow light to filter in through a second set of sheer coverings. Plush carpet made the room feel inviting and cozy. Every piece of beautifully carved furniture screamed extravagance. Oak finishes made each surface from the vanity to the bed posts glisten in the light of the chandelier above my head.

The plush bed I lay on, enormous and ornate, would've taken up my house's entire living room. A veil of translucent curtains hung overhead with a canopy that sparkled in the light streaming through the window. The sheets on the thick mattresses were pure white with golden, scroll designs across the covers.

My focus wandered to the window where daylight poured in.

How long was I asleep?

Instinct compelled me to search for my phone to check the time before—

"It's about time you woke up."

Erick's voice broke the silence with a crack and I whirled toward him leaning against the doorframe. Instantly, my attention flashed toward my appearance, hiding myself from him until I realized I still wore the same dress from yesterday. Relief swept over me and came out in a sigh as I relaxed against the headboard.

"Where am I?"

"My chambers, actually. You fell asleep and I didn't know where else to bring you." He rubbed the back of his neck sheepishly. "I'm not sure how you could fall asleep on the back of a dragon, but alright."

Rapidly, my thoughts searched through the night for any memories of falling asleep. I could only remember flying. My heart sank with a realization that I'd trusted him.

Stupid, stupid girl.

"What else happened?" I asked skeptically, subtly glancing at my dress under the covers to make sure everything was still intact. Aside from being a little ruffled from sleep, everything seemed well put together.

Still . . .

He watched me innocently, tilting his head in confusion of my underlying accusation.

"I let you sleep. I would've taken you back home, but I don't know where you live."

He pushed himself away from the door and approached me. I flinched, a spark of anxiety pressing my back against the headboard as he sat at the foot of the bed.

"Stay away from me," I ordered, my voice trembling.

Erick held up his hands innocently, his expression surprised. "Whoa, easy. I won't hurt you."

"Please." I shuddered, my skin prickling with memories of sensations. Hands touching me without consent. Forcefully making me comply. "Don't come any closer."

He watched me with narrowed eyes. "What else do you think happened last night?"

I didn't want to answer him. Instead, I covered myself with his thick, downy blanket and frowned. After a moment, he scoffed, his expression amused at first before shifting to horror.

"Tell me you didn't think . . . Good Heavens, Ellie, what kind of man do you think I am?"

I sighed, my nerves calming with the embarrassment that now flooded into my face. He shook his head and clearly tried not to laugh, his demeanor calm.

He's right. Of course he's not that kind of guy. That's my favorite thing about him.

"The kind I'm used to," I muttered, rubbing the goosebumps forming on my arms. His suddenly overpowering presence pressed down on me.

His eyebrows knit together curiously before a reassuring smile warmed his features.

Man, he has such a nice smile, I thought wistfully, allowing my heart to flutter a bit.

"I may be a 'player,' as you've so called me, but I would never take advantage of you or anyone else like that. You should know that," he said.

The words tormented me as I remembered who I talked to. I should've known that. I should've known a lot of things I didn't.

I could see it in his eyes. He wouldn't hurt me. At least . . . not like that.

Desperate to change the subject, I let my eyes graze over the breathtaking room with renewed awe. The air smelled woodsy and fresh, leaving me feeling cozy and safe. I wanted to let myself melt into the bed and bask in the heavenly atmosphere around me.

Erick gazed at me as if trying to figure out a complicated puzzle, his expression calm before.

I tried not to show how uncomfortable his scrutiny made me feel, though avoiding those piercing eyes proved increasingly difficult. Finally, I allowed my gaze to wander, meeting his.

"What?"

Erick's smile broadened for an instant, driving me insane, before he stood, heading for the door again and speaking over his shoulder.

"You're welcome to wander the palace and its grounds, though I'll caution you to stay out of the village for now, if you can."

I sat up straighter, my eyes darting around the massive, quiet room. Everything seemed close and overbearing. I didn't even want to imagine finding my way around the palace.

"Why?" I asked, tossing off the covers and following him into the hall.

He stopped and faced me, briefly searching the lavish hall for eavesdroppers.

"Well," he began, "I'd prefer to be there with you, for one. And Tyral doesn't exactly get a lot of visitors, so I'm not entirely sure how they'll react if you wander through the streets on your own."

I hadn't thought of that, though it made sense.

"I do have some business to attend to," Erick continued, glancing nervously at a tall clock standing against the wall.

"Like what?" I pressed. Depending on what it was, it could've given me a clue as to where he was in the story. Maybe I could help somehow.

He sighed, giving me a playful look and lightly tapping the tip of my nose. "Matters I'm not allowed to discuss with a subject."

I glared at him, folding my arms and leaning into my hip. "What's classified to the writer?"

He stared at me in dumbfounded silence. I could almost see the wheels turning frantically in his head as he thought up another excuse.

I smirked, knowing there wasn't one. I'd written enough scenes of him in council with his father and advisors to know what they probably talked about anyway.

Reluctant, he looked over his shoulder at a guard standing beside his parent's chamber next door. I felt his fingers land on my spine and I shivered away from him as he led me back into his chambers and shut the door.

"Have you written anything about the fires that have been happening lately?" he whispered, leaning close to ensure no one could hear, though we were alone. My heart jumped at the intensity in his deep eyes.

I had. How could I tell him though when he caused them? He didn't realize what he'd done, but he'd done it all the same. His red dragon slowly took over and he had little to no control over his actions while in that state.

I couldn't tell him. If I did, he'd be wracked with guilt and be constantly terrified every night for the rest of his life.

"Fires?" I asked, feigning innocence. "What kind of fires?"

He sighed, obviously disheartened by my pretended ignorance.

"I blackout once in a while at night and I don't know what's happened. There have been times where I wake up to a fire I didn't remember starting. I don't know if it's me or if there's another dragon we're supposed to be hunting or if someone is starting fires to urge on a war between Tyral and me. But it's been the main topic lately and the villagers are, understandably, frustrated and scared."

My heart sunk. I hadn't expected the story to be that close to its climax. I watched him, silently praying I wouldn't be around to witness any of those burnings myself.

"What's being done about it?" I asked.

Erick chuckled, leaning his head against the door again with a shrug.

"What *can* be done about it? The timing of my blackouts is too convenient to ignore, yet no one's seen the person or dragon responsible. Some villagers have been trying to rally an army to fight the dragon while others are trying to say it's our responsibility. 'We already have an army,' they say." He scoffed, shaking his head. "It's true, but what am I supposed to do? Turn myself in and lose the confidence of my people? I've already fought to gain their trust. Or do I have to continue this charade until I'm killed by my own people? Either way, it seems like I'm the villain."

I sighed, remembering what it was like to work through his storyline. For a long time, I didn't understand where it was meant to go myself.

He was right. He would be the villain in his people's eyes no matter what. I made the situation a bit of a no-win for him. It was meant to keep the momentum of the story going. Conflict was what made a story. Without it, there was nothing but fluff.

Erick's eyes darted toward a large, grandfather clock in the corner of his chambers and he flung open the door.

"I have to go. They can't start without me," he muttered, solemn as he gestured for my exit before him with a bow. "You're free to wander the palace and its grounds, though I still advise staying away from Tyral."

Chapter 8

"Erick crouched so the guards wouldn't see him eating his mother's favorite berries."

~ *Ellie's Story*

The pale golden Great Hall reflected itself off the granite floors. Light from the magnificent chandelier overhead illuminated the atmosphere with warmth as I wandered into the center of the hall to get a closer look. Thousands of crystals dangled around the candles inside it.

Two staircases climbed up the wall on either end of one massive flight of stairs. Railings of dark oak encircling them. I sighed, slowly making my way to it, though it was a workout just to get to the steps.

Purple banners hung on either side of the railings. I grabbed the corner of one, holding it out to look at it.

A crimson dragon's long tail wrapped around the stem of a rose. Its eyes stared directly at me, giving me a sense of uneasiness.

That was the symbol of royals in Tyral and the same picture as my notebook's cover.

I shuddered, nervously excited by their eerie similarities and haunted by foreshadowing. No wonder Erick reacted to my notebook the way he did. The similarities to his dragon form and the one depicted on the banner was uncanny.

Dad would've loved this.

I wanted to see more. I wanted all of it. For him. I owed it to him. I wanted my story, my world, my characters. It was all so beautiful. Yet, my stomach ached with regret.

My eyes wandered to the top of the staircase, legs moaning at even the thought of climbing them.

Turning to the large doors leading to the gardens, I made my way outside, my heels clicking noisily across the granite and echoing through the colossal room. Maids dusting various surfaces turned to stare at me, confusion on their faces. I put my head down and walked faster.

Relieved to finally make it outside, I sighed, leaning against the painted brick of the palace. Any embarrassment from my loud exit melted away once I saw the breathtaking landscape.

The grounds of the palace radiated beauty from every angle. The landscape of waning green blended into autumn. Red, orange, yellow. Fountains trickled water into large pools of stone. Erick's mother, Queen Lillian, loved fountains, so she had about a dozen of them placed around the gardens. Various fruit dangled from branches overhead, berries growing on the bushes I brushed my fingers across.

Glancing at the guards standing watch not far away, I picked a berry and popped it in my mouth. Its foreign taste filled my senses and I whimpered from the delicious sensation, my knees melting beneath me. I hadn't eaten since lunch the day before.

A chicken patty and mashed potatoes from school.

The very thought of food made me want to collapse from hunger. I nearly crumbled to the ground as I tossed more berries into my mouth, trying to seem inconspicuous and watching the guards. They surveyed the palace grounds, but didn't seem to notice me.

I could almost hear Monika ridiculing me for skipping meals again.

"You need to get your head out of the clouds and learn how to take care of yourself."

I rolled my eyes, though guilt pricked my conscience. I turned toward the forests surrounding the castle.

Did I come from there?

My world felt like centuries away from where I stood. That, however, was probably on account of the Victorian, Regency, and Medieval inspired atmosphere that surrounded Tyral. I'd always been fascinated by those time periods, though Mikey thought I was ridiculous for it. He chose to focus on the negatives such as a lack of indoor plumbing and nothing really fun to do. I, however, adored the simplicity and beauty and elegance the periods brought into the world.

My heart always yearned to be placed in an alternate reality. I craved the formality and grace that palpitated through the air when I thought of those time periods.

Yet somehow, I felt out of place in that world. Like a little girl playing dress-up. A fly on the wall. An observer among all the beautiful surroundings. I always thought that, if I could only step into Tyral for a minute, I'd become a different person. More confident or something like that. Instead, I felt just as lost and out-of-place as ever.

If I didn't fit right in Taylor's Grove and I didn't fit right in Tyral, where could I fit?

I turned skyward, the aftertaste of the berries bitter on my tongue with a sickening assurance of reality.

Monika is going to be so mad when I go home.

My dress tugged on a bush's branch, urging me to stay still. I couldn't sit still with the anxiety building in my stomach.

How will I ever explain my way out of this one?

"You're gonna kill me . . . or send me to a mental hospital," I muttered, thinking of my mothering sister with dread sinking into me.

I couldn't tell her about Tyral. I couldn't tell anyone. No one would really believe me unless they saw it themselves. Even then.

No one would believe me.

My heart raced, quickening my breath with every beat. I was going to be belittled for this. Ridiculed. Snapped at. Everyone would think I was crazy.

Am I crazy?

Yeah, I am. Look at me.

I gathered my skirt in a clenched fist, trying to calm down. Closing my eyes, I tried combating the accusations I imagined Monika throwing at me. Accusations she threw at me before buzzed in my subconscious, growing louder and louder until everything else was drowned out. Mom's disappointed looks clouded the blackness behind my eyelids. The sinking feeling of guilt surrounded everything around me, making what seemed bright before now darkened.

Irresponsible.

Cruel.

Selfish.

All those words snapped at me, different faces associated with each one with the nasty memories of who'd labeled me.

I turned toward the castle's turrets stretching into the sky, hoping to distract myself. Erick had been inside one of them for the past hour trying to figure out a solution for the fires.

I sighed, my conscience screaming at me like Mom.

I knew exactly how he'd be feeling in that meeting. Stuck. Hopeless to help with the situation. Scared to die and scared to live.

He'd likely be out soon. That thought lifted some of the anxiety for the wrath of my sister. I stood, trying to will my legs to move me toward a destination. Home, the forest, the palace. *Anywhere.* If Erick didn't come out soon, I'd run back home before Monika—

"Beautiful, isn't it?"

I whirled around at the sound of Erick's voice, my heart thrashing against my chest.

Chapter 9

"Taste Heaven or embrace Hell,

Trapped in a dragon's skin you'll be."

~ Ellie's Story

Air came and went too quickly, leaving my lungs unsatisfied from the restriction of a corset and anxiety. I pressed a hand to my chest with an exasperated laugh as Erick approached me, surprise in his startled eyes.

"Stop scaring me like that," I snapped, playfully slapping his chest with the back of my hand. He laughed, cringing away.

"You're so scare-able though." He grinned and popped a berry in his mouth.

I laughed emotionlessly and tucked my loose hair behind my ear, embarrassed by my over-reaction.

"Shut up," I muttered, turning to walk away from him. He followed, standing closer than I wanted him to. I felt his arm brush my shoulder as he strolled beside me. I hated that it made me blush.

"What were you doing out here?" he asked, breaking some of the tension lingering after our banter.

"I was just . . ." I hesitated, trying to think of an excuse. "Thinking."

Erick leaned against the trunk of a nearby willow tree, crossing one leg over the other. "What about?"

"Nothing important," I lied.

He watched me skeptically. "Come on, Ellie."

I sighed, searching for something to describe as a diversion.

I loved nature. Something about it always inspired me more than anything else. That garden was the most well-kept piece of land I'd ever seen. The grass was lush. Flowers all full and blooming. Not a weed in sight. A clean cobblestone walkway led to the center where a fountain with four dragon statues spewed water from their mouths.

I cringed with regret again at their fierce expressions.

"Sorry about all the harsh dragon imagery," I said, turning to Erick. "I didn't realize just how many statues there were like that."

He shrugged, his gaze scanning the gardens. "Some bother me more than others. That piece is my favorite, however."

I squinted at him, trying to decipher sarcasm. He chuckled, glancing sideways at me with a playful smirk. He hated all the statues depicting dragons. He didn't see himself the way they looked in those statues. Intense, menacing, hateful. He didn't feel like it was an accurate representation of facts.

It would be him soon though.

A twinge of guilt made me rub at the goosebumps on my forearm.

"When I described this courtyard, my muse didn't think twice about it," I continued.

His expression turned thoughtful as he plucked leaves from the willow's dangling branches. "Your muse?"

The confusion in his tone caught me off guard. "Inspiration. The little voice in my head that nags at me to write at the most inconvenient times. Muse."

Plopping himself onto the palace steps, he squinted against the sun behind me. "I've never heard that idea attached to a word before."

I chuckled. "Yeah, it's what leads me to write descriptions of places like this."

"You described all this?"

Nodding, I brushed my hand across the branch of the weeping willow. My mind wandered as I watched how they swayed in the wind.

"Well, most of it," I corrected. "There are little details I hadn't thought of before. But as a whole, yeah. I described everything."

He glanced at the courtyard, speechless. "How?"

"What do you mean *'how?'* I just sat down with a pen and notebook in my hand and wrote," I laughed. "I hardly had any control of what came to me after my muse took over."

"I mean . . ." He gestured vaguely to our surroundings. "How could words turn into *this?*"

"Like this." I sat down beside him, clasping my fingers together on my lap. His leg touched mine and chilling excitement rushed through my body. Pointing toward one of the willow trees surrounding the staircase, I began. "See the way it bends and twirls in the wind? The slightest breeze can pick it up and carry it around itself and twine its branches together."

He looked at me, confused surprise in his creased brow. "How do you do that?"

I laughed at his compliment, noticing how relaxed he made me feel. After the near anxiety attack earlier, the subject of writing came as an enormous relief.

"Close your eyes and think of all the different smells, sounds, tastes, and feelings you experience with every breath you take."

He obeyed, squeezing his eyes too tightly. I smiled, charmed by his scrunched-up nose. For the first time, I noticed a few light freckles dotting the bridge of it. He'd spent too much time basking in the sun as a kid instead of studying.

"Well?" I pressed after a moment of listening to him breathe.

He shook his head. "I hear birds . . . Maybe smell the grass."

"What color is the grass? What does it look like, feel like, sound like?"

"Grass has sound?" He opened his eyes, staring at me like the thought never even crossed his mind before.

A laugh as embarrassingly loud as the bray of a donkey burst from me, though I tried covering it up with the back of my hand.

"What's so funny? Who thinks of this kind of detail?" he asked, a little defensive behind his own laughter.

"I do," I chortled. "I have since I was little when my dad would describe stuff to me. That was an exercise he used to teach me to help me see things in a different light."

The ease of that confession gave me a sense of comfort. I'd never shown that game to anyone. Not even Brock or Jennica.

Erick watched me, his attention captivated by something in my face. He was close. Too close. His expression softened as he gazed at me. I blushed, standing to avoid the feelings bubbling into my stomach with that captivating look.

"Try again," I ordered, crossing my hands behind my back. "Listen past the noise and see if you can hear it."

He sighed, though his focus never really left me. Silently, he pursed his lips as his gaze grew distant.

"Is it the rustling?"

I smiled triumphantly, patting his head like a child as I passed him. "Good ear."

His smile brightened, something new sparkling in his eyes. Casually, he leaned his elbows on the steps behind him, stretching his legs and crossing his ankles.

I opened my senses to the world surrounding me, trying to listen for new words to describe it. A breeze picked up strands of my hair, kissing my cheeks as I squinted against the sun's rays. The cerulean sky welcomed a limitless idea of eternity. No clouds distracted from it. Only a deep horizon of trees and breathtaking beauty. Pine trees surrounded Tyral, hiding it from the rest of the world. I breathed softly, allowing the fresh air of near autumn to fill my lungs with serenity. Birds chirped in the willows and nearby birdbaths.

"It's amazing how descriptions come to me so vividly here," I said, meandering aimlessly across the cobblestone. "It's like the air is carrying them to me as whispers in my ear. The breeze is tempting me to write them down through the rustle of branches and leaves."

Did I say that out loud?

My heart froze with embarrassment. I'd gotten carried away.

I glanced at Erick self-consciously and he watched me in a daze, his head tilted to one side.

"Wow," he breathed, seeming lost in a daydream.

"What?" I asked, hoping I hadn't made myself look stupid.

"*That's* what you came up with from looking at a garden?"

"Yeah. Believe me, a lot more descriptions float around in my head than anyone will ever realize."

"Ellie, I've stared at this scenery my entire life and never, once, have I noticed the things you have in only a matter of minutes," he observed, shaking his head with baffled awe.

I giggled lightly, feeling my cheeks flush. Though it was a compliment, it made me wonder if it'd been a bad idea to tell him about Dad's ability to describe stuff.

"Is this everything you imagined?" he asked after a brief silence, still seeming a bit dazed.

I brushed my fingers across another dragon statue. Memories of words I'd written flitted across my subconscious. I frowned and pushed them quickly away.

"You have no idea," I mused thoughtfully, gazing upward at the purple flags flapping in a breeze.

Erick stood, crossed his arms behind his back again, and approached my side.

"Am *I* everything you imagined?" he asked, his tone genuinely curious.

I swallowed, nerves pricking at the surface of my skin. "Wouldn't you like to know," I teased.

No way I'm telling you that. Nice try.

My focus wandered to the statues on either side of the palace steps. Dazed, I approached it.

Taste Heaven or embrace Hell,

Trapped in a dragon's skin you'll be.

A siren's song locks in this spell,

But love's true words will set you free.

My skin tingled with recognition, my bones shaking from their eerie familiarity.

Erick's curse.

Chapter 10

"He'd only wanted to prove him wrong. He didn't want this."

~ Ellie's Story

Why didn't Dad tell me any of this world was real? Why would he keep something like this from me? Was he worried I couldn't handle it? Did he leave because he didn't want to deal with telling me someday?

He wanted to keep something secret here. What was it though?

If he'd told me, maybe I could've prevented the curse altogether. If I'd known Erick and Tyral were all real, I wouldn't have written my story the way I did.

How long had Tyral existed? He spent most of my childhood telling me stories of Tyral. I always knew that I based my story off ones he'd told me, but how much of it was actually *mine?*

"As a matter of fact. . ." Erick's voice pricked my skin, making me flinch. I'd gotten lost in thought again. "I *would* like to know how accurately I fit the descriptions in your head," Erick teased, knocking his shoulder playfully against mine.

I recoiled away from him, folding my arms to block out the relentless thoughts shoving their way into my mind.

You weren't ever good enough for him. Your dad left because of you. You drove him away like you always do. He didn't want to show you this place. He was ashamed of you because of what you did to these people.

I squeezed my eyes shut, goosebumps tingling across my arms.

What part of Tyral did he want to keep from me? How would he even know how my story ended?

Who cares? You failed to help anyone, so it doesn't matter.

My heart pounded. I stared forward, unable to push away the pain jabbing my gut.

"Ellie?"

I didn't respond. My brain could only comprehend the frantic noise in my head. My muscles tightened. A breeze touched my skin and it felt like an attack on my nervous system.

Why was he trying to hide this from me?

Because he didn't really love you, Ellie. You're worthless to everyone. Used and good for nothing but to be thrown away.

"You're shivering," Erick observed, shrugging off his tailcoat and throwing it over my shoulders.

I flinched again, startled by the scratchy fabric against my skin. He tugged on his tunic sleeves as if the gesture was completely ordinary. I hesitated, staring at him. Instantly, all negative thoughts fled, replaced with endearing pride for the character I'd created.

No one's ever done that for me before.

How do I react to this? Thank him? Shrug off the gesture like nothing special?

The reaction that came to me was a tug of emotion burning behind my eyelids with unexpected tears.

In an effort to hide from it, I hugged the tailcoat tighter around me and turned away from him. I wanted to lock in the feeling of warmth and acceptance. Bask in the sweetness of the gesture.

A full grandeur of trees covered the pathway separating the castle from the village with speckled shade.

"Come on." Erick motioned for me to follow as he meandered forward, hands clasped behind his back and a gentle smile brightening his face. "I'm free for a few hours. I'll take you wherever you want to go."

I sighed, my focus wandering toward the world I'd been forbidden to venture to. A full grandeur of trees covered the pathway leading to the palace gates with speckled shade. A black, iron gate surrounded the grounds. I hadn't noticed that the palace sat atop a small hill until then.

I sighed, turning back to the palace, wanting more than anything to get lost in fantasy. But Monika would already ring my neck as it was.

"I don't want to go home," I moaned to myself.

"I'm sorry?"

I flinched, turning to Erick who stood ready to guide me wherever I wanted to go. Embarrassed, I waved off my words with a floppy hand.

"Oh, nothing." I looked at my fingers twirling awkwardly around each other. "I should get home. My sister is probably looking for me."

I shuddered thinking of the cold greeting surely waiting for me when I walked in my front door.

His expression changed for an instant. He opened his mouth to speak, but shook it away and shrugged, grinning sweetly and bowing grandly. "In that case . . . Please allow me to escort you, m'lady."

I blinked, unsettled by his willingness to let me go so easily.

"You're not . . ." I hummed, trying to understand.

You're not going to fight me? Insist I stay until your curse is broken?

He raised his eyebrows, waiting for me to finish. I smiled, tugging the collar of his coat closer to my chest.

"Thank you."

I'd never meant those words so much in my life.

I could've analyzed his behavior toward me. Wondering endlessly about his intent, how he thought of me, if he liked me . . . But for the first time in my life, I didn't want to. I only wanted to enjoy the fantasy for a while.

I smiled brightly as I passed, content until his fingers gently skimmed my waist.

His touch only lasted a second, but it seemed to singe my skin. Long after his hand left, I felt the presence of his touch.

The gesture was gentlemanly. Not explicit in the least. No expectation of anything in return.

What am I supposed to do with those sweet gestures?

I found myself staring at his profile as I walked beside him. His sleek, black hair glistened in the afternoon sun, tumbling over itself on his forehead above his dominant eyebrows. He squinted against the sun, crinkling his straight nose. He seemed deep in thought and a little disturbed.

I wondered if he thought about the council. Which one was it? Could I help?

Stop staring at him, Ellie.

He walked closer than he had before. A subtle change, but enough for me to notice his arm lightly brushing my shoulder every once in a while. He seemed to be unaware of the proximity, but it drove *me* nuts.

I stared forward. I really tried not to think about how his coat's fabric itched my skin when his arm occasionally brushed across my shoulder.

His stance was stiff as he walked with his head down, kicking pebbles along the way.

Look at literally anything else, Ellie. Stop staring at him.

Sighing, I let my gaze wander to my dress swaying around my feet. The dirt path, though partially paved, created a small puff of dust when the hem of my skirts swiped across it. I loved the feeling of petticoats against my leggings. I felt so old-fashioned and pretty in that getup.

I surveyed my surroundings once more while I still could.

Little things caught my eye that I hadn't thought to describe before.

Ellie, you don't know everything about this world. There are things Dad kept from you.

I shook my head, halting.

Erick kept walking until he realized I'd stopped and turned to me.

"Erick," I began, the taste of his name freezing my body with fear of his answer to the questions I had.

He looked at me and my throat felt dry. Those eyes. So clear and honest. Trusting. Open.

Guilt darkened my soul with the humiliating realization of everything I might've missed while writing.

"Yes?"

I swallowed stabbing nerves rising into my throat. "What's something about you that I might not know?"

He pushed air out in a gust, creasing his brow. I smiled, imagining wheels spinning in his brain as he searched for something.

"Umm . . . Like what? Don't you know more than I do?"

"I'm not sure. That's why I was hoping you could tell me," I said, hoping I didn't look ridiculous for not knowing everything.

He hesitated. "You already know my heritage. My curse, my current political situation, my backstory—Good heavens, you know my backstory."

The horrified realization in his expression made me laugh.

"Yeah, I know all about that, promiscuous Prince Erick," I teased. "Now tell me something I don't know."

His face paled and he stared forward in stunned silence. I wondered if he sorted through his entire past trying to find anything that he *really* didn't want me to know.

He probably doesn't want me to know any of it.

Exasperated, he groaned and ran his fingers through his thick, black hair. "I hadn't thought of that. I hope you don't think . . . I would never—"

I laughed again, though it stung a little. I tilted my head and rocked back and forth on my heels.

"You would *never* whisk me off into the night on a bet with your cousin that you couldn't get as many girls as he could?" I said, sarcasm in my tone. "You wouldn't take me to your room when I fell asleep, claiming nothing happened when really—"

Erick glared at me, confused and appalled. "Ellie, stop it," he barked, his expression more hurt than angry. Flinching, I hesitated, taken aback by his sternness. His eyes softened into sadness as he tossed his hand as if giving up. "Well, you *certainly* seem to know more than I do, don't you?"

I pursed my lips, shame for my assumptions pulled my focus away from his harsh eyes. I'd really offended him with that sarcastic accusation.

I knew he never did anything a girl didn't want him to. He wouldn't do that to them and he wouldn't have done it with me. Still, something heavy entered my chest, darkening my judgement.

When I didn't respond, he continued. "I made the mistake of using girls' affection to win a bet. But never, *once*, did I do anything against their will. The sorcerer who cursed me didn't know that either and mistook me for my cousin who got everything by force. My cousin didn't think it was possible to get a girl's affection through respect and genuine attachment. He tried to convince me that I was too safe and I couldn't get as many girls to fall in love with me as he could. He thought that my way was stupid and I wanted to prove him wrong. I accepted that bet because I wanted to show him that it's not how love works."

I frowned as I listened. He was right.

"Petegrath cursed you because he knew you were better than that." Those words rolled off my tongue before I could stop them. "He was disappointed that you'd be so careless."

I could feel the weight of my words on his shoulders as they slumped.

"I didn't mean for it to go on as long as it did," Erick confessed, his eyes cast downward. "I shouldn't have been that way. I think I let my cousin's influence get to me more than I should've. But since then, I've tried to be better. I've tried going back to how I was before. That's why I spend so much time in council with my father. Do you know how many of those I skipped because I was with a girl trying to get her to fall in love with me?"

I nodded.

"I don't want to be that way anymore. I've spent so long trying to distance myself from the person who accepted that bet."

My heart hurt as it reached out for him. I longed to soothe his suffering somehow. Let him know that he'd be okay. His pain showed so vividly in his voice and the way he hung his head.

"I'm sorry, Erick."

Those words tugged on my conscience. Their truth tickled my tongue. Burned in my core. I stepped closer to him. Getting hurt didn't mean anything to me in that instant. I only wanted to ease his pain. Let him know that he wasn't alone in the battle against his curse. Assure him of how much I cared about his situation.

Against everything inside, I reached for him. Stepping close, I allowed my fingers to graze his cheek to turn his attention to me.

His eyes met mine and sent a jolt of adrenaline through my system. They were *stunning* up close. My heart thrashed. His lips parted as his breath quickened, eyes glancing at my smile.

It took everything in me to allow my fingers to remain on his face, though I pulled back slightly. I felt stiff. Afraid to move and afraid to stay still.

"I'm here for you, Erick."

In that moment, I was ready to do whatever it took to help him. Even if that meant I got hurt in the process.

Chapter 11

"Melodies repeated in his thoughts as he analyzed them, imagining different sounds to bring his music to life."

~ Ellie's Story

His silence cut me. He seemed lost, confused. My entire body trembled with the physical contact. It was the first time I'd touched a guy like that for months. Mikey never liked being touched like that. Touching Erick's cheek felt intimate. Through that simple, yet meaningful, gesture, I felt connected to him. Drawn in by the coarse sideburn by his cheekbone and his deep eyes. Being so close, I could see the subtle detail of scales in his irises, an unsettling reminder of his curse.

Stupid, push him away like you have everyone else.

I bit down on the emotion suddenly tightening my throat. I hated that I'd caused him so much pain.

"Ellie, I'm so ashamed. I didn't care about them like I should've. They deserved better than—"

"Erick," I laughed, shaking my head as I pulled my hand toward my chest. "Shut up."

His expression turned unexpectedly serious and I frowned, his shame sinking into me instead.

"What will it take for you to trust me?"

"Umm . . ." The question struck me. He still thought I didn't trust him? "T—tell me something I don't know about you, I guess is a good step," I said, walking again.

He sighed defeat, sprinting to walk beside me again.

"I'm . . . a musician. Well, composer. I don't actually play a lot of instruments, aside from the pianoforte. Instruments were more my cousin's area of expertise."

Glancing over his shoulder for any watching eyes, he placed a hand on the small of my back to guide me to the palace wall. A break in the stone led out to a secret passage. I recognized that exit from my writing as the one he escaped through occasionally to submit to his curse.

He continued talking once we'd slipped out through the other side.

"I constantly have music in my head. It's always there, even when I'm not writing it down or playing it aloud." His eyes were a little playful as he smiled at me. "I believe we have that in common."

Hesitating, I watched him as we entered the forest. We did have that in common. His world plagued my thoughts constantly and there wasn't much I could do about it. Everything I saw, I couldn't help but silently describe. That sometimes made school and social interactions hard.

I hadn't realized, however, that he thought of music and composing constantly the way I did with writing.

Something strange happened inside me when I realized we had something like that in common. I was used to no one truly understanding that feeling.

All at once, the guy next to me wasn't just some vague idea I'd dreamed up as a fifteen-year-old. He was human. His own person apart from me that had thoughts, feelings, and actions of his own. He became more real to me in that moment than he ever had before.

I knew about his love of music, specifically the piano his father—

"My father gave me a beautiful pianoforte for my birthday that has been my most prized possession since I was a child. I fell in love with it as soon as I touched the ivories."

I smiled, watching him with a feeling of contentment washing over me.

Nice timing, Erick.

Maybe there were things about my world I hadn't thought of before. After all those years of writing, plotting, and living in Tyral inside my mind, what other kinds of things would I discover diving into it?

Erick held a tree branch above his head and let me pass ahead of him. Those gentlemanly gestures of respect ate at me bit by bit.

I looked up to see the fallen tree, a mixture of surprise and relief sweeping over me.

"We're here already?" I didn't remember it being so close. For an instant, I felt the sagging weight of disappointment weighing on my shoulders like sopping wet clothes.

Erick nodded, turning to me slowly and rocking back and forth on his heels. His eyes caught mine and he paused, breathing deeply though his parted lips.

"Ellie," he began.

I smiled in response, tossing my hair from my eyes and folding my arms.

"Umm, could I walk you home?" he asked.

His sudden shyness caught me off guard. He usually spoke so smoothly and seemed to know exactly what to say at exactly the right time. Instead, he shifted awkwardly from one foot to the other. It was endearing to see this side of him. I'd never really written him as nervous, especially when speaking to a girl.

Probably just because of who I am. Probably thinks I could smite him at any second and doesn't want to do anything stupid. It's not because he cares what I think or cares about me.

I nodded, appreciating his offer.

He glanced at my hand before meeting my eyes again, cleared his throat, and indicated the fallen tree.

"Ladies first."

I climbed onto it, my skirts making it difficult to maneuver around the trunk.

"Ellie," Erick coughed as if he'd held it in since the castle.

I turned to him, tossing back my sandy hair. His spine stiffened, mouth open to continue. Obviously afraid to continue, he cleared his throat way more than necessary.

"What?" I urged.

"When you said you'd be there for me, what did that mean?"

I hesitated, trying to think of a way to explain myself.

"I'll help you . . . No matter what."

He blinked, his expression contemplative as he lifted himself onto the fallen tree.

Lavender smoke surrounded me as soon as I landed on the other side of the fallen tree. When I looked down again, I was back in my jeans and T-shirt.

Some part of me resented the lighter weight of my street clothes as opposed to the heavy fabrics of a gown. I felt almost naked and thrust into reality. One I didn't want to face again.

Erick walked me home in silence, for the most part. He brought up little details about the forest that he said he'd never noticed before, watching me as if for approval.

When we reached my back yard, I felt like a two-ton weight sat on my chest with the hefty dread pulsing through me.

"I, umm . . . So, what exactly will breaking the curse entail?" Erick asked, breaking the silence between us. He released a quiet moan as he twisted his neck, wincing at the pain.

"What's going on?" I asked, my hand reaching to rub his neck. The instinct caught me completely by surprise and I froze, my hand hovering awkwardly over his shoulder.

"I'm fine," he spat.

His tone was like a slap in the face and I pulled my hand back. My heart fell with the realization of what I'd promised.

What if I can't do this?

His curse is only going to get worse if he doesn't really fall in love with someone before it overpowers him.

"Can you tell me how to break this curse?" he asked, his voice strained as he rubbed his neck.

"It's . . . complicated," I said, hoping he wouldn't press me just then. I didn't want to explain it.

His snappy tone set me on edge and I backed away from him.

Wincing, he sighed. "I'm sorry. I shouldn't have snapped at you. The moon is getting fuller, so the curse comes on earlier."

I rubbed my arms, hoping to block out the chill of those words.

The brighter the moon, the stronger the effects of his curse.

"I better just . . ." I muttered as I turned toward home.

"Ellie," he called after me. I looked at him, tucking my hair behind my ear. His mouth pulled to one side in a playful smile. "Meet me here tomorrow morning."

My body froze with the invitation. I couldn't think of anything to say or do in response other than wave awkwardly and walk away.

"Bye, Erick."

Chapter 12

"Family approval meant little to him . . . Until it was all he had left."

~ *Ellie's Story*

You've killed an entire kingdom, Ellie.

That thought shot into my subconscious like a bullet to my heart. My eyes shot open, disappointment sinking into me when I woke up on the purple pillow Mom and Dad bought for my birthday the year he left.

Was it all just a dream?

I sighed, tossing off my covers and getting out of bed to get ready for another uneventful day at school. My eyes flashed to the notebook Dad gave me, its hand-crafted cover facing upward. Something about it left me unsettled. I picked it up and flipped through it, opening up to the bookmark to indicate a spot I wanted to look over again.

I still remembered vivid details of my dream. When I went to write it down, however, its descriptions already met me on the page.

I hesitated, still drifting back into reality after waking. Maybe I'd dreamed about what I'd already written down.

It'd never been so vivid though. I remembered every little thing, the sound of wings against the night air, the taste of wind, the crisp atmosphere of endless sky.

It was all there. My eyes scanned over the words written clearly on paper.

I had to have dreamed about writing. Not the other way around.

Shaking my head out of a haze, I combed my fingers through my hair, unintentionally yanking on an untamed knot.

"Ow," I moaned, my voice hoarse.

Muscles in my spine yelled at me as I stretched, my reflection in the mirror startling me. My hair wasn't usually that stringy and messy in the morning and I still wore the T-shirt and jeans I'd worn yesterday.

How'd I get home last night?

I couldn't remember anything except my dream of flying on the back of my fictitious dragon and visiting Tyral.

How'd I end up back in my room after going to the bookstore?

A sinking feeling of guilt for something I'd written the day before.

What was it again?

All at once, my bedroom door opened and Monika stood with eyes wild with terror. I couldn't decide if the exasperated sigh that burst from my older sister implied relief or intense anger.

I squinted at her, my vision still a little hazy. "Hey, sis, what time is—"

"Where *were* you?" she snapped, approaching me for a tight embrace. I stepped back in surprise.

"What do you mean?"

I was thinking the same thing, sis.

The way she hugged me was either affectionate or violent. I couldn't pinpoint which. She squeezed so tightly I grunted from having my lungs squished.

"You scared the life out of me. Where were you?"

I opened my mouth to answer, but hesitated, my brain scrambling for something to cover for my lack of memory. When I couldn't come up with anything, I resorted to my generic excuse.

"I—I went to Brock's."

He'd always been pretty good at covering my tracks when I'd snuck out before.

She pulled away and glared at me. "He didn't know where you were either. I'm not stupid. You were out with Mikey again, weren't you? Ellie, why can't you stay away from him? You know he's a jerk."

I glared. "I haven't seen him since my birthday, thank you. I learned my lesson."

"Have you though? Because I'm beginning to wonder if you *can* learn lessons, Ellie," she shouted, narrowing her eyes back at me. "When are you going to grow up and learn how to take care of yourself? You're eighteen, you're going to have to learn how to be responsible and stop being such a child."

I flinched with the sting of her words.

Her expectations of my behavior had always exceeded my age. She expected me to act *her* age even though she had nearly four years of experience over me.

I didn't want to respond to her accusation. Instead, I took it. Gritted my teeth, and took it like the pathetic little wimp I'd always been. My heart plummeted with the weight of those thoughts, plaguing my conscience with the aftermath of destructive words thrown at me. I didn't know how to fight with her since she always won. If she didn't, it meant another week of bitter silence and passive aggressive comments thrown in my direction.

Pulling black curls over her shoulder, she folded her arms and pressed her lips together.

"Aren't you going to answer me?" she snapped. "Were you even listening?"

Her sharp tone stabbed me like a dagger, her words sinking in and turning the knife.

"I have to get ready," I muttered, pushing her out of my room with a frown as deep as the pain I felt.

"For what?"

"School."

"It's Saturday."

I paused, blinking with confusion. “It was Thursday yesterday.”

“No, you’ve been gone since Thursday night when you went to the bookstore. When Jennica and Brock didn’t know where you were, I almost called the cops. I wasn’t about to call Mom when she’s on a business trip.”

I pursed my lips in frustration.

Just like Mom to put the fear of God in Monika if she dared interrupt her while working.

“And if her daughter disappeared like her husband, she couldn’t spare a few minutes out of her precious lifestyle to—”

“Don’t you dare say that. That’s disrespectful and rude and—”

The sting worsened. “And selfish, and inconsiderate, and hurtful, and a plethora of other terrible things, right?” I mumbled, hoping she wouldn’t hear me.

“Come on, Ellie. Stop being so dramatic. You’re acting like Dad.”

“Good, at least one of us does.”

She hesitated, deescalating the volume of our fight. For an instant, a sense of pride beamed inside me at the thought of finally rendering her speechless. That feeling quickly diminished, however, when I noticed the moisture in her eyes.

“There’s a lot you don’t know about Dad,” she muttered, glancing cautiously at the door, subtly checking for Luke as an eavesdropper.

“Like what?”

She stared at me and, for a minute, I saw vulnerability in her through the walls she’d created. I caught a glimpse of myself in her. I understood her. She had just as many hurt feelings as I did.

It only lasted a second, however, before she shook it loose and returned to her usual, critical demeanor.

"Never mind, you wouldn't get it anyway," she grumbled.

Insulted, I shook my head.

"Whatever. Mom wouldn't come back even if I'd been lost in the woods for weeks and they found my remains."

"Get over yourself already. You're not the only one who suffers because of what happened to Mom and Dad, Ellie."

Her words crawled into my heart, piercing me to the core and twisting my gut into a mangled heap of emotional stress. Did she really have so little respect for me?

"You certainly wear your grief well then," I retorted under my breath, shoving past her and rushing for the back door to hide from my shame.

Tears welled in my vision. When I blinked, one drifted down my cheek and I instantly swiped it away. I couldn't handle the amount of hefty words she thrust at me anymore.

I slammed the door shut behind me, purposely leaving my phone behind. No way I wanted her calling or texting me after that one. She'd never leave me alone.

Monika's voice echoed in my thoughts, relentlessly thrashing against every part of me until every nerve in my body deadened to the cruel words.

The worst part of it, I knew she was right. I just didn't know how to change myself enough to finally earn her approval.

Maybe I'd never earn it.

Maybe I didn't want to.

Chapter 13

"Maybe he'd find the words of his curse somewhere in there."

~ Ellie's Story

My legs carried me to the forest on autopilot. I ducked around tree branches and climbed over roots and stones dotting the ground. The trees seemed to shout at me, relentlessly looping her destructive words.

Get over yourself already.

Wiping at tears, I hiccupped. My heart heavy with my sister's words pressing on me. I didn't even know if what she said about me was true or not. I only knew that it hurt.

I kept walking until finally reaching the fallen tree.

I didn't have much time to breathe a sigh of relief at being there again before memories flooded my thoughts again.

Not a single one of them, however, related to Dad.

They all revolved around Erick, Tyral, the palace, and . . . the dragon.

Nerves peeked and I swallowed, approaching the tree cautiously. I wasn't sure what I'd find on the other side. Maybe nothing. I hoped that wouldn't happen. My heart pounded with anticipation as I peered onto the other side.

At the sight of him on the ground, leaning against the trunk of an aspen, I sighed and my knees wobbled under my weight with relief. I had to support myself against the fallen tree to keep from collapsing.

I'm not crazy then and I wasn't dreaming . . . He's real.

His head of black hair faced downward as he stared intently at a book on his lap. One leg stretched out before him, the other bent.

As casually as I could manage, I rested my chin against my palm and watched him.

He looked so peaceful and contemplative as he read. Words I'd crafted before formed involuntarily in my head.

He knit his brow, trying to follow the antient text of the book of legends and spells. Maybe he'd find the words of his curse somewhere in there. Histories and legends, fact and fiction. They blended together after a while.

"What're you reading?" I asked.

He flinched, his focus shooting toward me.

"Ellie." He scrambled to his feet, snapping the book shut and tripping over the leaves covering the ground beneath him. His clumsy fumbling made me laugh. "I thought you might've forgotten me."

I brushed hair from my vision. "Of course not." *I just thought maybe I'd dreamed you up.*

The grin on his face gave away more about his thoughts than he probably meant to reveal. He was genuinely happy to see me.

"Wh—what book were you reading?"

He glanced at the book in his hand and chuckled a little uncomfortably.

"Just some history on magic in Tyral," he said, approaching me beside the tree. Seeing my character walk toward me felt surreal. I couldn't decide how I felt about it, but instinct pulled me back. "It's more like legends rather than history. Most of them revolve around the sorcerer, Petegrath."

"Find anything interesting?"

Erick released a hefty sigh and approached the fallen tree. "Nothing too interesting in here."

I tilted my head curiously, unsure what he meant.

"Anything interesting *outside* of that book?"

He met my eyes with a playful smirk.

"Besides your pretty, blue eyes?"

I narrowed them in response to the cheesy line and shoved his shoulder. "You can do better than that."

He laughed, turning his attention back to the book in his hands.

Standing so close to him in street clothes when he wore tunic and trousers felt unnatural. Yet, exhilarating. It seemed like I was merely a bystander to him. Watching a historical fiction movie where the main character interacted with me.

He leaned his arm against the wall of trees, flipping aimlessly through the pages of his book.

"There really isn't much in here aside from stories of times he's protected the kingdom. Apparently, he created this wall to hide Tyral from intruders and probably from nosey little girls snooping around their back yards looking for trouble."

He lifted an eyebrow at me, smirking. His teasing didn't strike me as funny.

"Petegrath made the wall of trees?" I asked. "Why?"

"Really, Ellie, you need to know this stuff." He gave me a sideways glance before flipping casually through the book again.

I sneered at him, lightheartedly batting my eyelashes at him like an innocent little girl and leaning my chin in my palms.

"Maybe I'm just making conversation," I bantered, mimicking the words he'd said to me on our first meeting.

He blinked, something subtly shifting in his expression as he searched my eyes. His chest rose and fell with a deep sigh as his spine stiffened.

I'd affected him.

He stared into me briefly and something inside shifted.

Oops.

I hadn't expected flirting with him to come so naturally . . . Or to have such a visible effect on him.

He released his breath slowly, his mood seeming completely altered before he cleared his throat and tore his attention away.

"I've tried to remember the words of the curse, but little pieces have escaped me."

I hesitated, trying to remember his curse myself. I always had been bad with poetic writing.

"I'm hoping you can give me some sort of insight," he continued.

The lump in my throat swelled when I tried swallowing past it. "How could I do that?"

He stared at me a minute, confused. "Don't you have it written down somewhere? Maybe the notebook you showed me in the bookstore the other day?"

Panic rose in my chest when I spat the word, "No."

He would never read that notebook. No one would. Unless I sent it to a publisher and editor to fix it up and make it pretty, I'd never let anyone look at it. And what if he read the ending? He didn't know what would happen to him. If he found out, how would that affect him? Or the story?

He couldn't know.

"Why no? How else am I supposed to remember what that old man said?"

He'll die. He doesn't remember. He can't change it. The only way he can is by falling in love. That doesn't happen in the story.

I watched him, trying to hold in my thoughts as he stared at me intently.

I promised him I'd help him . . . No matter what. That means I would have to let him fall in love with me.

"Just . . . trust me. You don't want to read your own story," I muttered.

I can let him fall in love with me without getting too involved myself, right?

Chapter 14

"He thought she meant so much to him. But he couldn't hurt her by pretending anymore."

~ *Ellie's Story*

"Are you ready to see your kingdom?" Erick asked, pulling himself onto the fallen tree. He reached for my hand to help me up. I hesitated, remembering my promise. I needed to do whatever it took to save him. I had to let him fall in love with me. If I kept rejecting him, how could I do that?

Tentatively, I took his hand, letting him guide me along the fallen tree and help me down on the other side.

I closed my eyes, basking in the lavender magic that would change my appearance to match Tyral's style of clothing. Relief swept through me with the idea of stepping away from intrusive sisters, ex-boyfriends, and anxieties of everyday life to absorb fantasy for a while.

When the smoke dissipated, I met Erick's gaze. His expression relaxed as his head slowly fell to one side. A gentle smile teased the corner of his mouth, his silver eyes deep with contentment. They sucked me in, tugging on a piece of my chest that'd been blocked out to the world for months.

"What?" I asked, a little entranced by his smooth expression. *He's so much more attractive in person.*

His smile grew as he stood a little taller, gradually tugging me toward him by our clasped hands.

"You're very pretty, Ellie."

My spine stiffened and I frowned. I didn't push myself away from him, though we stood closer than we ever had before. Erick's hands encompassed mine, his thumbs resting comfortably on the backs of my hands. Warm and inviting. *Too* inviting. I wanted to stay near him. I wanted to hear more stuff like that. It felt nice to hear genuine compliments like that.

My body felt jittery, panicked, and unsettled. I couldn't seem to stop moving, hounded by those words as I slid my suddenly sweaty hands from his and wiped them across my dress. I folded my arms and unfolded them again, confused about where they were supposed to rest naturally. Nothing felt natural except the instinct to run. I didn't want to run. I wanted to stay with him. I wanted to keep allowing him to hold my hands in his like that, but my body's response went against everything my heart wanted.

Protect yourself, stay away. Go. Get away. Run. Get out of here.

As if to distract myself from those thoughts, I fidgeted with my hair.

"Just take me to Tyral, please," I said, ducking my head and wrapping my arms securely around my torso to hold me together.

Stupid. Why can't you just let him hold your hand and compliment you. It's so simple. Let him fall in love with you just so his curse will break and no one has to get hurt.

I winced.

Everyone will get hurt. That plan is terrible.

It's the only way to break his curse, Ellie.

He can't fall in love with me. He's gonna mess up the story. I'm going to ruin the story if I keep letting him rope me in like that.

"All I said was you're pretty," he stated, his voice wary as he approached me again. "Am I not supposed to think that?"

Before he could come any closer, I threw my hand out, landing straight onto the center of his bare chest, exposed beneath his V-neck tunic. My heart leaped as I stared dumbly at my fingers.

What're you doing, Ellie?

The skin peeking from just below his collarbone was smooth and firm beneath my trembling fingers. A hint of his chest teased me as I matched my breathing with his. His heartbeat pulsed against my fingertips.

How dumb do you have to be? Stop it!

I wanted to feel his pulse more. Soak in the calming reassurance of his existence. He was real.

His breath touched the back of my hand when he looked down at my hand. I couldn't bring myself to take my hand away, no matter how much my thoughts discouraged that kind of physical contact.

It was *so* wrong. He was my character. Fictional. A girlhood fantasy. But if he was, why did he feel so undeniably . . . *real?*

I'm in way over my head here.

How could I let him fall in love with me in good conscience? Knowing that I wasn't ready for him. I never would be ready to fall for him too.

But I was going to keep it platonic.

Then why is your hand on his chest?

He wasn't supposed to find anyone he really loved. That was the whole point. It was supposed to be a narrative on what love really is.

Disappointing.

Devastating.

My story wasn't supposed to be a love story. It was more of a tragedy.

The world froze for an instant. In spite of myself, I couldn't seem to look away from my fingers fumbling with his tunic's frilly collar. Sensations I'd never experienced before pulsated through my veins with every heartbeat. I couldn't think about anything except how pleasant his skin felt against my palm.

Slowly, his fingers grazed my wrist, his piercing silver eyes darting to my face . . . down at my lips. He stepped a little closer. Timidly, my fingers curled, gathering fabric, as I found myself coming closer and allowing my focus to wander to his lips.

We hesitated, mere inches from each other. His expression turned dazed as his attention darted across my countenance as if asking permission to get closer. Close the gap floating between us like a cloud of thick fog.

Stop it, Ellie. Don't interfere in his story.

His eyebrows knit together, hope in his eyes.

Wow, his eyes are stunning.

Erick's tentative movements drew me in against my better judgement. I closed my eyes, breathing him in. His skin reminded me of a home I never had. A dream I'd always reached for but never caught.

I tensed, releasing my grasp with one swift movement as I stepped away, awkwardly pulling my hand to my chest. Embarrassment flooded my cheeks when I realized that I'd involuntarily tugged him toward me. My heart throbbed with a sharp intake of breath.

All at once, I was transported to the night of my last birthday. Mikey kissed me the same way. I took him back that night. It was also the night I found out he'd cheated on me with several other girls.

The sinking in my gut left me feeling like shmuck. Used. Dirty. Unworthy. Useless.

Panicked, I woke up, pushing him back and unable to look in his eyes.

You're vulnerable, Ellie. Don't trust him. He's going to hurt you. You're not part of the story. Quit butting in.

He held my gaze as if waiting for my response before he reacted.

"Sorry," I whimpered, stepping away and trying to catch my hastened breath.

"What happened? Are you alright?"

"Just . . . Please don't do that again."

Leaning against an aspen, I shut my eyes and sighed, allowing the piney, familiar scent of trees to peel away at my feelings and tug them out of me.

"You are so infuriatingly intriguing." Erick's voice cut through my peace.

I flinched, whirling around to face him. Silently, I rubbed my forearm, unsure how to respond to his observation.

Please, don't push me, Erick. I can't do it. I can't handle this. I'll go insane.

"Yet, the most infuriating thing about you is how much I want to keep digging deeper into your mind."

"Please, just . . ." I hesitated, stopping myself before I said something stupid. "I'm really not that intriguing," I said. "Please don't act like I am. I'm just a confused girl who can't decide whether to live in a fantasy or reality."

He shook his head, a tired smile relaxing his features as he approached me. "I'm still a fantasy to you?"

I sighed, feeling physically drained from trying to fight against the idea anymore. "No."

He chuckled, approaching my side again and leaning against the tree, crossing one leg over the other with folded arms.

With a wicked grin, Erick tilted his head. "Then where's the conflict?"

Hearing that tugged on my heart with panic.

Everywhere.

"Come with me to Tyral, Ellie."

I felt my face relax into a smile as he pushed himself away from the tree and began walking deeper into the forest. After a few steps, he turned, walking backward as he gestured for me to follow. I looked homeward, memories of Monika's words flashing vaguely across my subconscious. I winced, looking at Erick again. His smile caused a wave of calm to sweep through my body.

In that moment, he seemed more like a home than I'd ever had in Taylor's Grove.

Chapter 15

"Stone, dragon heads haunted him at every angle. They were so vicious."

~ *Ellie's Story*

Erick pushed against a cloud of branches, not leaving my gaze to reveal a spacious field of colorful wildflowers. The colors encircling the field caught my breath and held tightly. Long, yellowing grass, purple lilacs, foxtails, and dandelions waved in the breeze, carrying their flowery sweet scent on the air.

Behind a massive stone wall in the distance, the castle stood on a tall hill. Steeples, drum towers, and turrets extended into the turquoise sky, bartizans resting on the sides of its tan walls. The castle was about all I could see from where we stood, but that was enough to make me feel weak at the knees.

"I don't believe this," I breathed.

Erick grinned broadly, a satisfied gleam in his eyes.

"Shall we?"

He gestured with a deep bow and placed one hand on his chest, the other gesturing for me to go before him.

My heart raced and I grinned with excitement, hiking up my dress's hem to maneuver through the field. He walked close beside me, but not in a way that implied possessiveness. In a sweet way like he genuinely wanted to be near me.

"Erick," I sighed, pressing a hand to my bosom and gathering my pale gold skirts with the other.

"What do you think?" he asked.

I laughed aloud, choked by the emotion tight in my throat. "It's exactly how I imagined it."

A triumphant smile beamed on his face the whole way toward the wall surrounding the kingdom.

"I thought you'd say so. It is beautiful. This is the field where I wake up every morning. The first couple of times I changed back, I woke up in the castle courtyard completely exhausted. Luckily, guards or servants weren't around at that time and the ones who were didn't see me . . . As far as I know." We looked at each other and embarrassment colored his cheeks. "I'm sure you already knew that though."

I laughed nervously at a spike of insecurity, brushing my fingers over the yellowing grass grown to my knees. "That doesn't mean I don't like hearing you tell me."

He chuckled, holding his arms crossed behind his back. "Is there anything you don't know?"

Pausing, I combed through everything. The storyline, plot twists, character arcs. I seemed to know all of it I nodded before an image came to my mind of one of Erick's final transformations and I shuddered. I could almost hear his screeching as fire poured from him in blazes, consuming everything in his wake.

"I don't know," I mused.

I found Erick's eyes again and tried to distinguish how much time he had left based solely on the shade of his irises. If they were red in the least, that meant he was coming to the book's climax. But if they were still silver, he had time. He glanced sideways at me and I breathed a sigh of relief. Silver. Clear, happy silver.

"Are you enjoying the view?" he asked snidely with a mischievous grin.

Drawn back into the moment, I blinked. "What?"

Erick laughed. "You're staring at me like I'm a piece of art."

"No, I'm not."

"Then explain why you're still doing it."

I'd been caught again.

Flashing my gaze downward, I frowned, pushing my way ahead of him without saying anything more.

Everyone around me probably thought I had an unnatural obsession with them because of how much I liked people watching. I liked trying to figure people out by simply observing. Though I'd been yelled at several times for getting carried away in my own thoughts. People didn't like being watched.

Subtly, Erick took my hand to lead me toward a narrow alleyway leading to the village square. Out of instinct, I slipped my hand out of his. He paused.

"You really don't like that, do you?" he observed, watching me with curiosity.

I shook my head. "I told you, I'm just not used to it, that's all."

His gaze turned sympathetic before he peered around the corner where a narrow alley began, the arrow-loop cut big enough to fit one person at a time. It opened straight into another thin alleyway between the tall, stone walls.

Vaguely, I remembered Erick passing through that place in previous story entries. It was much more claustrophobic than I'd originally imagined.

Once we reached the mouth of the tunnel, I looked up and saw the castle perched atop the hill, stunning against the cerulean sky.

"Follow close behind me," he whispered.

My heart skipped a beat with the excitement bubbling in my stomach. He bit back the grin creeping along his countenance before leading me through the secret corridor just outside the square that he snuck through every morning.

What if Tyral isn't as beautiful as I pictured it?

What if the people there treat me badly?

There were a few people in that kingdom I knew wouldn't like me if I ever had the crazy opportunity to meet them. So much so, I joked about it with Brock once when we were younger. He agreed with me since he'd read my story and knew who I referred to.

I was a rural, modern girl coming into a fantasy world filled with legends, gowns, and magic.

What if I fail to match up?

You're only playing dress-up.

I held my head high, inhaling deeply.

I don't care. I'm not about to let stupid little "what-if" scenarios intrude on this opportunity.

Erick's demeanor relaxed as he snuck around the wall beneath a large flight of stairs, placing his hand on the design of a dragon's head, its mouth open and eyes wild with fury.

Though an amazing decoration, it still made me grimace.

He glanced at it, cringing as he released his hand and rubbed his fingers together as if to brush off residue.

His eyes darkened as he muttered, "I've never felt comfortable with how many dragon heads surround this kingdom. It makes me feel hunted."

I flashed him a sympathetic smile, remembering a section I'd written about how trapped he felt living in the palace.

You are hunted, Erick. You just don't know how that plays out for you . . . yet.

I watched him in silence for a moment, my thoughts wandering. He smiled back tiredly. When was the last time he'd gotten enough sleep?

Some villagers didn't trust him, for legitimate reasons. He'd been caught a few times in the past sneaking around at night with girls. Though he didn't do that anymore on account of his dragon form, they still saw him sneak around the castle walls so he could shape-shift in peace.

Hardly anyone in the village knew about his curse . . . Except for Jerome. He actually witnessed the prince's change once, though no one believed him.

"Anyway," Erick said, gesturing vaguely and breaking our eye contact. "Welcome to your kingdom, Ellie."

Chapter 16

"Some villagers disturbed him with nightmares of being hunted."

~ Ellie's Story

The kingdom had never been that huge in the buildup of the story. Necessary, but fairly insignificant to the overall plot. A crowd of villagers bustled around us. Two kids ran past me as they rolled a wooden wheel with a stick down the road, laughing and calling out to each other in a game of Hoops and Sticks.

Aimlessly, I wandered until my back hit against the brick wall of a building.

Erick laughed lightly, a charming twinkle in his eyes as he brushed his hair from his forehead. It bounced back with a cowlick in the center of his hairline. Dazed, I watched him, words forming in my thoughts without my permission. It glistened in the late afternoon light, creating a sheen across the top of his head. The crease in his cheeks complimented his stunning smile. Crinkles framed his eyes, making them shine with bright happiness.

He rubbed the back of his neck.

I swallowed the spike of adrenaline I felt. I meant to turn away. Instead, I found myself gaping, my focus falling into an all-encompassing daze.

The bustling world behind him made me feel dizzy with a strange sense of familiarity. Strange, in a world so unfamiliar. Seeing him facing me seemed completely unreal as he approached me.

"Anything to say?" he asked with a snide chuckle. "You're staring at me like you're in a trance."

I blushed, meaning to turn away from him, but unable to. I couldn't quite wrap my brain around reality yet.

"It seems so . . . *real."* I brushed my hand across the window frame of the building I leaned against. The rough texture of the wood scraped gently across my fingertips with a familiar feeling that reminded me of the fallen tree back home.

"That's because it is," Erick commented, a playful lilt in his tone. "Tell me something I don't already know."

Noticing the wording of a question I'd asked him earlier, I leered at him and nudged his shoulder with mine when he joined me against the wall. He returned it and grinned, bowing his head.

His hair dangled forward, resting across his forehead again when he turned back to me.

"I love it, Erick," I said, crossing my legs over each other in front of me as carriages clamored across sandy terrain. "It makes me want to write, more than anything."

He turned his attention to me, his expression relaxing into contentment. "Why write when it's all here in front of you?"

My thoughts scrambled for a legitimate reason until I sighed, watching a couple pass by, their arms linked together as they strolled the square.

Once I started talking, my mouth ran off without me.

"Well . . . Back home, whenever I'd see a physical place that reminded me of something I'd imagined before, there's an urge to capture the scene with words that completely takes over my thoughts. My fingers start twitching to write down the descriptions I feel inside me and it's difficult to leave that alone. It throbs in my head sometimes until I have a headache and the only way to really get rid of it is through writing. It's like a life source for me sometimes. I couldn't function without it."

His calm demeanor betrayed something deep as he listened, thoroughly involved in every word. He blinked slowly, subtly adjusting his position to close the space between our shoulders.

"Indulge me with descriptions in your head . . . What're you thinking?" he urged, a tone as smooth as honey.

Folding my arms, I cleared my throat and turned toward the crowd, though I could hardly think about anything but the way he looked at me.

I didn't want to answer him. My mind drew a blank and I shuddered under his intent scrutiny.

Ignoring his request, I continued on a contemplative route. "I probably should learn how to control this overpowering urge to always have a pen in my hand. My best friend, Jennica, says all the time that I'm too obsessive and I need to get out of my head more. She makes fun of me sometimes for how often I zone out when talking to people because I can't help but notice stupid things about how they look."

Erick chuckled, his arms folded across his chest. "Is that why you stare at me all the time?"

I hesitated, horrified that he'd noticed. "No." He gave me a knowing look and I swallowed, sighing in defeat. "Yes."

"And how do you describe me?" he asked, seeming lost in thought.

After thinking for a minute, I sighed and flipped my hair out of my eyes. "Well, it's from your perspective, Mr. I'm-going-to-dominate-every-scene. So, there's honestly not that much description of you in it."

I wasn't lying, technically. There weren't that many descriptions I'd written down. Yet, in my head, I'd described him a million times over. Subconsciously, I studied the way he moved, how he dressed, how he talked. The little crinkles in his cheeks when he smiled. How he rubbed his neck whenever he felt nervous.

Erick creased his brow, faking offense and placing a hand over his heart as his jaw dropped. I laughed.

"How dare you say such a thing. You shouldn't accuse your prince of such arrogance."

Playfully, I pushed his arm and he laughed with me, pulling away and rubbing the spot.

"Answer my question," he pressed, lightly tapping my temple. "You have to have several different words to describe me in that pretty little mind of yours."

I clasped my fingers together and placed them on my lap, giving his appearance another once over.

In a word, handsome. Possibly the most attractive guy I've ever imagined, let alone met.

You'll never know that though, I mused, determined to believe it.

The way he looked at me might've made me want to swoon if I hadn't known better.

His silver eyes shimmered with his relaxed smile, giving a warm and welcoming air of confidence I'd never seen in someone before. His confidence was natural, unlike Mikey's whose façade often crumbled when faced with getting caught in a lie or when something didn't go the way he wanted it to. Erick's presence felt honest and open with a willingness to listen to whatever I had to say.

I'd never met someone so similar to the guy I'd always dreamed about but never thought I'd meet.

My thoughts wandered back to how I would describe him and I smirked, avoiding the question to look through the window of the shop we leaned against. As soon as I did, I gasped.

Different types of swords, javelins, and knight's armor hung on the walls. Bows and crossbows hung on a separate wall, quivers filled with wooden and steel arrows sitting beside them.

"Oh, if only Brock were here," I muttered, not realizing I'd said it aloud until Erick responded, his tone a little on-edge.

"Brock?"

I flinched, facing him beside me. "My best friend. He'd love all the archery equipment. He'd probably know more about it than I would."

Erick's demeanor stiffened slightly and he exhaled slowly, looking in beside me.

A tall young man with long black hair sat on a chair inside, carving the handle of a beautiful crossbow. He lifted it to admire his work and I caught a glimpse of his face.

He was handsome with high cheekbones, dark eyebrows, and bright blue eyes. The handle of the crossbow in his large hands had engravings on it that swirled around the arrow, the trigger in the center of a beautifully carved rose.

"I've had a couple of swords made by the hand of Myron. He's been creating swords and armor for our guards and soldiers for nearly thirty years. His son, Jerome, is quite a talent, though his specialty leans more toward archery equipment rather than blacksmithing. He's been working on an arrow to tranquilize any beast it hits long enough to haul them away unharmed. I've been trying to convince him to join the royal guard so they'll have something to shoot me without killing me."

I shuddered. Jerome was a character I'd always been fascinated with and had contemplated writing a spin-off story about. Maybe tell the story of when he'd seen Erick shape-shift.

Erick didn't know about that. It was why Jerome crafted the Mystic Arrow.

"You're dodging me again, Ellie," Erick teased. "How do you describe me?"

Slyly, I gave him a side glance and gravitated toward the door to the shop. A bell beside the door announced me as I entered and Jerome looked up immediately.

"Welcome to Myron's Armor and Equipment," he said, looking twice and lingering with wide eyes the second attempt. "Oh . . . h—hello, Miss." He stood quickly and the freshly carved weapon toppled to the floor.

"Let me help you—" I began, crouching to pick it up before my corset restricted me.

He picked up the crossbow quickly, staring at me for a second before smiling coyly and clearing his throat more than necessary.

"No, that was my fault." He stood too fast, slamming the back of his head on the slanted ceiling. He grunted, rubbing the spot he'd hit.

I laughed, covering my mouth to suppress it from coming out too loudly. He smiled at me, probably happy he'd made me laugh.

"I'm Ellie," I said, holding my hand out for a more formal greeting.

He stared at my hand with creased eyebrows for a minute before taking it and kissing my backhand.

"Ellie," he said thoughtfully. "A fitting name for one so fair."

I blushed, a bit uncomfortable with the compliment as I slid my hand from his.

"My name is Jerome. I'm honored to make your acquaintance," he continued after a second of questioning silence.

It was nice, for a change, to run into people who practiced such polite manners. No wonder Erick was so awkward and out-of-place in Taylor's Grove.

"So . . ." My thoughts turned to the arrow Erick mentioned. The mystic arrow was meant for him, since Jarome had seen Erick change. He didn't want to kill the prince, but he wanted to capture the dragon to impress Dawn, the village beauty.

"How can I assist you today, Miss Ellie?" he asked, a little more collected.

I glanced over my shoulder at Erick speaking to someone out of my view before leaning close to Jerome.

"I need you to do something for me," I whispered, cringing at my wording. "I mean, the prince."

His brow creased with curiosity. "Umm . . . Yes, ma'am?"

"Eri—the prince—told me you're working on an arrow that penetrates, but doesn't harm the one shot," I began.

He narrowed his eyes at me suspiciously. "With all due respect, Miss Ellie, that is confidential information I'll only discuss with the prince himself."

"Trust me." I shot another glance at the door, feeling urgency pulse through my system. "I have the best interests of the prince at heart."

His eyes shifted like he didn't quite believe me, but was too polite to say anything.

"Find the sorcerer Petegrath. He's the only one who wields magic in the kingdom anymore and your only hope for making that arrow a success."

Jerome stared at me, his expression blank with confusion. "I'm sorry, Miss Ellie, but he's been gone for several years. No one really knows what happened to him."

I hesitated, trying to remember writing that. I nodded when the scene of Erick's curse being cast came to me. He'd been trapped in a book when Erick's cousin reflected a spell directed at him with a mirror.

How had I forgotten that detail? I hadn't looked at that specific part in so long, it seemed almost irrelevant to the story itself.

"Right, he hasn't been seen since . . . Jerome, how long has the sorcerer been missing?"

"About five years, Ma'am."

Five years. Why does that sound so familiar?

The bell above the door announced another entrance. I whirled around, my heart launching into my throat when Erick walked in, his smile bright. Jerome's spine stiffened and he clamored back awkwardly.

"You're into archery and weapons, then?" he asked lightheartedly. He approached me, standing so close my shoulder brushed against his chest. His strong presence made me feel petite and feminine, though my heart felt heavy with questions. "You're certainly full of surprises."

"Your Majesty." Jerome bowed.

Erick grinned insincerely, seeming a bit annoyed by the formality. His hand touched my waist, sending chills down my spine with his careful and slow movement. I shriveled away from the jolt of exhilaration it caused.

"How's that arrow you were telling me about?" Erick asked.

Jerome stiffened and fumbled for words, glancing at me with a nod so subtle I almost didn't notice. "Father is still testing it. We've yet to find a formula that works properly. All the other attempts have failed, but I'm hopeful."

Erick's mouth turned up to one side in the smallest smile I'd ever seen on him. "Keep me informed on its progress, but be careful. Have you told anyone else?"

Jerome glanced cautiously at me and Erick followed his gaze. "She can hear this," he assured quickly.

With a raised eyebrow, Jerome tilted his head. "She can know, but the king can't?"

"Trust me, Jerome, she's more involved than you'd think," Erick said.

The scent of fresh pastries wafted with a breeze. I turned to the door where a bulky woman with the build of the high school's cafeteria lady stood in the doorway, two little boys at her sides. One munched on a jelly-filled pastry while the other clung to the woman's hand, sucking on his thumb. I recognized the woman as Mila, a seamstress, and her two sons, Tyson and Rick.

Beside me, Erick's spine stiffened and he shot in a quick breath. He leaned closer to Jerome, his tones softened to a whisper. I couldn't quite hear what he said, but I was too captivated by the new company.

I knew what happened to them in the story. Their fate seemed solely my responsibility.

Tyson and Rick were so much cuter than I imagined. Rick's dark hair sat messy on his head, eyes big and cerulean as an ocean. Tyson's blonde hair and brown eyes was a trait he acquired from his father who'd died two years prior. His expression was serious as he gripped onto Mila's apron.

"Come now, Tyson, you're gettin' it all over," Mila griped bitterly, bending down to scrape the jelly from his cheeks. "How many times do I have to tell you? Food goes *in* your mouth."

I chuckled at that, enchanted by them. I couldn't seem to take my focus away. They seemed a part of me.

I couldn't tell what it was that drew me to them, but before I could think twice, I approached them.

Chapter 17

"Erick froze. Something wasn't right with her."

~ Ellie's Story

"Excuse me. . ." My hand found Mila's broad shoulder and she whirled around dramatically. Her hazel eyes widened as she pressed a hand to her large bosom. She stepped back, examining me critically, a laugh in her voice.

"Oh, my . . . Who might you be? I haven't seen a new face in this kingdom for years."

I smiled, extending a handshake. "I'm Ellie."

Her eyebrow raised skeptically. "What strange mannerisms. Where'd you come from?"

I hesitated.

"Ummm. . ."

How could I answer that? I hadn't thought of a proper response yet. I'd only been in the kingdom a few hours and I'd already messed up. I swallowed through my dry throat, heart pounding as I stumbled over words.

"I—uh . . . What sweet little boys," I said warmly, gesturing to Tyson and Rick. They hid behind their mother's dress, their expressions wary with childlike shyness that warmed my heart. As a signal of trustworthiness, I smiled broadly at them and knelt to their level. They tucked further behind Mila, nervously tugging on her petticoats to shy away from me.

"What's your name?" I asked, reaching out for Rick to Mila's right.

"Rick," he responded meagerly, popping his head out like a jack-in-the-box.

"I'm Ellie," I said.

"I'm Tyson," he piped up, clearly jealous of the attention given to his younger brother. I turned to him and laughed. "I'm six." He came out from behind Mila, his chest puffed out with pride at being the eldest.

"Wow, you're practically a man," I exclaimed enthusiastically.

A smug grin brightened Tyson's features as he turned to his brother. Rick slowly braved approaching me, sucking on his adorable little thumb.

Something in my heart expanded when I was around children. Nothing made me feel more fulfilled than getting a frightened child to open up to me. Something about that made me feel like I could accomplish anything.

Someone tapped me on the shoulder. When I turned around, Tyson stood behind me, his cute little six-year-old mouth pursed tightly with jealousy.

"Rick is four," said Tyson matter-of-factly, his consonants blending together with innocence.

"You're both so big and strong. Hey, you guys want to see a magic trick?" I asked, plucking a loose button from my dress sleeve. Dad taught me several growing up, though I only remembered one or two.

The boys gathered, Rick leaning on my shoulder to get a closer look, the sound of him sucking his thumb directly in my ear. It was the cutest noise I'd ever heard. It reminded me of my little brother, Luke, when he was that age.

"How dare you say such a thing to my children," Mila snapped, grabbing their shoulders and shoving them behind her. "Who do you think you are?"

I craned my neck to look up at her. I'd forgotten about her abhorrence of anything pertaining to witchcraft, as she referred to it. I swallowed, realizing I'd just made an enemy.

"I—I'm sorry," I whimpered, fiercely intimidated by the rather large woman now towering over me with bulky hands on her hips. I stood quickly, tucking my hair behind my ear and staring at her in terror.

Really smooth, Ellie.

I hadn't expected her to be so upset. I struggled to think of anything to say when someone took my hand. I flinched, turning to find

Erick slipping it into the crook of his elbow in one smooth gesture. The forced smile on his face warned me to get away. Fast.

Mila grinned too much, her eyes guilty once she clearly realized I was associated with the prince. Her changeable mannerisms gave me whiplash and reminded me of Mom.

"Oh, Prince Erick, you're far from home, aren't you?" she said, inclining her head and bowing so deeply she nearly sat on the ground.

Tyson and Rick hid behind her again, cowering. Erick responded with a slight bow in return, a hand resting on his chest. She straightened, resting a hand on her thick waist and tilting her head at him in an accusatory manner.

"It's lovely to see you again, Mrs. Oscar. How's your cat?" Erick said warmly, appearing sincerely interested in hearing the answer.

"Dead."

I blinked.

Well, that took a dark turn.

"Oh, I'm so sorry to hear that," I said, genuinely sorry to hear about the loss of her cat since I loved them so much.

Mila clasped her fingers together, ignoring me. "Where's your guard, Your Highness? They shouldn't be letting you roam about without . . . protection."

Instinctively, I stepped away from the piercing glare stabbing us with her unspoken threat.

Clearly uncomfortable, Erick laughed loudly, his grin too broad and incredibly nervous. "I do apologize, but if you'll excuse us . . ." Erick pulled me the opposite direction without acknowledging Mila any further.

"Your Highness," Jerome called out before the door shut behind us.

I stared down, watching the swish of skirt around my feet as we walked briskly away.

I never expected a character in Tyral to act so hostile. I'd certainly never written that woman so intimidating. Facing her in person felt very different from what I'd expected. I knew she was intense and far too involved with the royal family's matters, but she was much more frightening than I remembered.

Erick's arm wrapped around my waist and he leaned close to my ear, his breath tickling my neck.

"I'm sorry for that," Erick whispered. "She's the biggest advocate in the kingdom for killing the dragon. She terrifies me."

"I can see why," I retorted. "I never expected such a rude welcoming. I guess I thought they'd all know who I was like you did."

He chuckled, bowing his head to people passing, smiling politely and making direct eye contact with most. Vaguely, I remembered a sentiment Dad taught me that I'd thrown into Erick's character.

Smile at everyone. You never know what people are going through.

"I only knew to look for you because of my curse and a legend my cousin told me about."

"But since I'm the writer, can't I make them do whatever I want?"

His laughter spat from between his teeth with an apprehensive edge. "That's a frightening thought . . ."

Instantly, my mind wandered to what kind of power I wielded. I could make anyone in this kingdom do anything I wanted them to. But if I did, what can of worms would that open? The story was already written. Could I really change *anything* about it?

"I doubt, however, that you're constantly writing about me and my people, so what happens then?"

I shrugged in agreeance, trying not to think about how closely he walked to me. His arm left my waist and part of me missed the security it gave me.

It's a false security. You're not safe with any guy . . . except maybe Brock.

I shook the thought away, pushing my hair behind my ear.

His focus wandered skyward at the setting sun and he winced.

"I better get you back home," he commented. "I have another council to attend."

His hand landed on my spine as he guided me out of the streets. The touch shivered through me and pricked my skin with a flash of memory that tampered with my senses. Stiffening, I decided to grin and bear through the painful memories his touch evoked.

You have to stop being so afraid of him. You want to help him, don't you?

I sighed defeat, forcing myself to relax, before Erick glanced at his hand and pulled it away.

An instant sting of regret and guilt shrouded my thoughts.

Why is this so difficult for me?

Chapter 18

"The room seemed darker when he entered, covering the air with the scent of danger."

~ Ellie's Story

Erick walked me home before I realized how hungry I was. Even the thought of Monika's chicken curry made my stomach rumble. My car still sat in the bookstore parking lot. So, driving somewhere wasn't an option unless I wanted to walk to the bookstore first.

I shuddered. I wasn't ready to go home. Being home reminded of Monika's destructive words. Seeing my bedroom window brought me back to the moment she started yelling at me. Those words still pranged against my skull, nagging me for attention. I didn't want to give them that. Regardless, they seeped into my skin and lingered there, trapped by the rising goosebumps.

To get away, I walked, intending to head for my car before my stomach gurgled at the scent of garlic bread and pasta wafting in the air.

I didn't realize I was so close to the quaint, Italian café, La Ciliegia in Cima, or *The Cherry on Top.* Brock, Jennica, and I went there every so often when one of us needed a pick-me-up. It was our favorite place to eat other than Jennica's house.

A small bell above the front door announced my presence as I passed the threshold. I closed my eyes and basked in the delicious scent of the chef's famous pizza. A waitress greeted me and I opened my mouth to tell her to seat me for one when a voice cut in behind me.

"Two, please."

I froze, my spine tingling as his hand brushed across my waist. He tugged me toward his muscular torso, his fingers gripping the small of my back. I shriveled away. He only held tighter. His laugh rumbled deep in his throat laughing as he pressed me securely against him.

"Sorry I'm late, babe." Mikey's voice slithered through my body and I shuddered. The kiss he threw onto my cheek made me flinch and pull away. "I'm sure you'll understand."

I didn't want to believe it until I turned around to see his devilish grin. When I saw it, I froze with terror at the reality of him.

"We've got a little catching up to do," he said to the waitress in an alluring tone. If I hadn't known to look for it, I would've missed the wink he gave her. My stomach turned with nausea as panic settled in. "Is there a *private* booth you could give us?"

Staring wide-eyed, I silently begged her to give us a table in the center of the empty room. I wanted at least one witness if I found myself trapped by him again.

Instead, the waitress eyed him, smiling like a submissive puppy bowing to its master. She looked at me, jealousy and judgement in her subtle glare.

I cringed.

I'd lost the war again and stood utterly alone. In that one look, I knew Mikey had her under his spell and I didn't have a prayer.

"Of course." Her voice had a bite to it that I recognized after dating Mikey for so long. She hated me. "This way."

"Thank you, Lindsay," he said, placing his strong hands on my shoulders and pretending to rub them. In reality, he didn't want me to get away. His grip ached in my arms, but I knew better than to resist in public. He'd make me pay for it later if I did.

She led us to a booth in the back corner of the restaurant, as far from the kitchen and witnesses as we could be.

Panic pounded through me like I was being led to the gallows.

The world slowed down and my only thoughts revolved around trying to understand my situation.

My heart pounded with adrenaline. I hadn't seen or heard from my ex-boyfriend in eight months. I was finally over him.

Why'd he show up *now?*

"How's this?" the waitress, Lindsay, asked, her voice sickeningly sweet.

"Perfect," Mikey chimed in. "Like you."

I almost rolled my eyes. *You can do better than that, Mikey.*

Regardless of the cheesiness of the grooming, she giggled.

"Let me know if there's *anything* you need," she insisted, flashing me a snooty side glance before walking away.

Once she left, Mikey sat me down then planted himself beside me, trapping me in the booth. I stared forward, avoiding eye contact and forcing my brain to remember what those hands rubbing my back were capable of.

"How are you, Ellie Belly?" he asked, tickling my stomach.

I flinched, remembering how he'd told me to lose weight if I cared about him. Almost starved myself to make him happy, yet he never was.

The feeling of his touch finally awakened my senses to the situation I was in. I lurched away from him, slapping at his hand.

"Don't touch me," I growled, glaring darkly at him.

Mikey's eyes widened with surprise like me fighting back gave him immense pleasure. "Oh, you don't want to be tickled?" His strong fingers prodded my sides and I curled away from him, wanting to yell. Do *something* other than give in.

"No," I barked, trying to show in my tone how serious I was.

"Come on, just a little. . ." He leaned toward my neck, the smell on his breath reeking of day-old vodka. He was sober, but forgot to brush his teeth again.

I froze, sighing with the weight of exhaustion. I didn't have the energy or will to fight back just then. He wouldn't stop anyway and just become more forceful until he got what he wanted.

"What're you doing here, Mikey?" I asked dully, trying to envision being in the forest again as his lips grazed the side of my neck.

"Ellie," he purred, reminding me of a serpent.

"Here to beg me to take you back again?"

He stopped and pulled away, a frown deep on his face. His expression of disappointment sparked feelings of inadequacy. Like I'd betrayed him by speaking my mind. Without any forethought, my heart sank with the realization that I'd let him down again. I wasn't *cooperating* enough.

The logic in my head told me to roll my eyes and shove him out of the booth. The emotional side ached with the guilt of not just giving him everything.

His brow furrowed and he scooted closer to me, his eyes dark as he cornered me with an arm draped around my shoulders.

"Take you back? C'mon, Ellie, you're smarter than that. How can I beg you to take me back if I never really left?"

I gaped at him, unsure what that meant.

"What are you talking about? You left me after you cheated on me with three other girls . . . At the *same time.* On my *birthday.*"

He chuckled low in his throat, shaking his head as if scoffing at a misbehaving child he couldn't help but adore. His fingers caressed my cheek as he said, "I'll always have control over you, even when I'm not around."

Those words stuck to my skin like pine sap. "What does that mean?"

He chuckled. "I know you, Ellie. You're predictable. I'll always know where you are. You're never *really* alone."

I rolled my eyes, though his words still left me unsettled. "Whatever . . . Then where have you been the past eight months?"

He tilted his head in feigned innocence, blinking slowly. "I've been giving you space, but I've always been there for you. Isn't that what you wanted?"

"No, that's what *you* wanted the first time you cheated on me."

"C'mon, sweetheart." His fingers brushed down my neck and tugged on the collar of my shirt. Anger and fear spiked inside me and I slapped his hand away, my spine stiffening. "Everything I've ever done was for you—"

"Get off of me," I growled, finally gathering the courage and energy to shove my elbow into his chest in an effort to escape. "I told you not to touch me."

"Shh . . . Ellie, don't fight me," he said, his voice calm as he cupped my face in his massive hands to force my stillness. He made me look him in the eyes and instantly, my mind went blank.

"Ellie, what happened to you? You used to be so warm and affectionate. You liked when I touched you before . . . I miss that . . . I miss *you*."

I glared at him, hating the exhilarating thrill shivering through my body when his fingers brushed across my bare skin. I wanted to hate the intoxicating allure in his brown eyes.

His appearance hadn't changed much. Thick strands of dark hair dangled over his temples in front, the rest cut short. If I were a stupid girl, I would've melted at his deceitfully charming smile, framed perfectly in dimples. He wore the leather vest I'd bought him a few years before, bulky arms exposed through the ripped sleeves of a white undershirt, showing nearly every tattoo he sported. Part of me wanted to relish in the fact that he'd kept it all that time.

His face was scruffier than before, but still not enough to qualify as significant facial hair. He never could grow it out.

Horror struck me when I realized his roguish charm still drew me in.

Chapter 19

"He couldn't find even a moment of rest on the night of a full moon."

~ *Ellie's Story*

You meeting someone here?" he asked, his expression cloaking possessive jealousy. I stared at him, shaking my head as disappointment seeped through my skin. *He's not good for me. He'll never change.*

"If I was, you forfeited the right to know things like that eight months ago."

He scowled, placing one and on the table and the other behind me as he leaned over me with a suddenly dangerous presence. I shrunk into the booth corner. That look always preceded intense spurts of anger, usually resulting in a bruise.

"I'll always have a right to know, Ellie," he whispered, a threat hovering in his tone. "Now, tell me before I make you."

Instinct told me to cower. Hide. Obey. He would do anything to get what he wanted. If he did, it usually meant taking advantage of someone somehow. He never played fair.

His presence made me feel as vulnerable and submissive as if I stood before him wearing nothing but the skin of my back.

"No," I snapped, surprised by my own courage. "I don't even know what you're talking about."

Mikey chuckled low in his throat. "I know ways of making you croak, sweetheart." He pushed a calloused finger below my chin, tilting my head up. He opened his mouth to speak, but hesitated, his grin amused. "What if I asked Jennica? Then what would you do?"

I glared at him. "Don't touch her, Mikey," I growled, the need to protect my best friend overpowering my intimidation.

He shrugged nonchalantly. "If you don't do what I say, I can't promise you anything. I'm sure she'd be more willing to cooperate than you ever were."

"Stop it, Mikey," I growled, though his threat wielded so much more power.

"She's known for giving *amazing* results with very little work since she's so *easy*."

The calluses on his hands from fights and guitar strings scratched my cheek as they caressed my jawline, subtly surrounding my throat.

"All I would have to do is suggest that maybe you'd been lying to her. After all, if you were really her best friend, how could you not tell her? She'd want to know if you were involved with someone who could be potentially . . . dangerous." His fingers tightened around my neck as he laughed. "She'd tell me *anything* I asked her to if I did it *nicely.*"

His touch left me trembling, feeling fragile and bendable like he could break me in half with one twitch of his long finger. I pursed my lips.

"Please don't, Mikey. Stay away from her."

His eyes widened and he pulled away, laughing and biting his tongue with sharp incisors. "Yeah," he purred, pulling my head toward him. "I always did like your feisty side. Show me more." His fingers wandered toward my collarbone, sliding lower.

Instantly flashes of memories scattered across my brain in a flurry, shooting warnings against the center of my chest.

Get away. Run. Do something. Don't let him do this to you again.

I remembered the last time he'd done that. Finally, a burst of anger pressed my hands against his chest and shoved him back. He only grabbed my wrists and yanked me onto his lap. Panic surged through me with the shock of pain in my wrists and shoulders from the force.

If there were ever a time to fight back . . .

I jabbed my elbow into his gut with a burst of adrenaline. He grunted, but still held fast to me, eyes fiery.

"Try that again, sweetheart, and see if it works out for you," he hissed, his grip tightening.

I clenched my fists so hard they turned white. Fear made my skin numb. It made everything numb.

He stared into my eyes for a minute, searing into my soul with guilt I'd become all too acquainted with.

"Try it again, Ellie," he barked.

He squeezed my wrists tighter, digging his fingernails into my skin until slits of red colored his fingertips. I winced, whimpering from the pain. I only wanted freedom.

"Tell me who he is and I might let you go—C'mon, Ellie Belly, why are you so scared? Who are you meeting here?"

Something rang in my ear. His voice overshadowed any hope of escape I had as I crumbled, cowering to him once again.

Idiot, fight back!

Mikey leaned closer, his voice a low hiss as he whispered, "You're a tramp, baby girl. No one will ever love you like I did so you should've been grateful for what you had when you had it."

Someone called my name, though I could hardly hear anything through Mikey's threats and degrading comments.

He looked up, laughing as he let his head fall backward.

"Oh no, Ellie Belly. *Him?"*

"Get your hands off her," growled Brock as he shoved chairs aside to get to us faster.

Everything blurred together as I watched Mikey stand from the booth, scoffing. Brock glowered at him with blood lust in his eyes. I'd seen that look only once in him before when Mikey cheated on me the first time. If he could've shot an arrow through my ex-boyfriend's chest, he would've.

"I *knew* it," Mikey snapped, shoving his hands into Brock's chest. "I knew you loved him. You always trusted him more than me. C'mon, Ellie, you left me for this weak, pathetic imp who could never stand up for you?"

In one swift movement, Brock grabbed Mikey's shirt collar. "I told you to leave her alone then too."

"Brock, just stop," I pleaded, panic freezing my bones.

"Guess I don't blame you," Mikey continued, "I mean, who can resist such a cute face?" He puckered his lips, squishing Brock's cheeks between his fingers as he laughed. Biting his lower lip, he raised his eyebrows, silently daring Brock to do something about it.

Brock's fist swung. Mikey's head tossed to the side and he held his jaw, wiping his mouth. With a deep growl in his throat, he lunged at Brock.

"Stop!"

I put myself between them before I could think twice.

The fist in my gut stole my air. I hardly felt the pain through gasping. Blackness shrouded my vision for an instant and I was on the floor, coughing and gripping for any air I could muster.

"What happened?" Lindsay, the waitress, ran from the kitchen, a hand pressed to her chest.

I squeezed my eyes shut, but heard Mikey shout, “Why’d you hit her, Brock? She’s my girlfriend.”

Vaguely, I noticed Brock’s fingers tighten on my shoulders as he helped me stand again.

I wished I had the words to spit back at him. Instead, I only glared at him.

“Get out, Mikey,” Brock ordered.

Mikey scoffed before the fire in his expression died down, replaced with smugness like he’d just won a wrestling match.

“Fine, if you want to be that way,” he barked. “Forget it. Cheat on me all you want. You’re not worth it.”

I didn’t even feel pain through the relief following the intense shock of his drastic change in demeanor. It took me a second to catch my breath and bring myself back into reality from the haze of adrenaline.

Then shame entered the hollow place in my chest that seemed reserved for the pain he caused.

I let him down again.

Chapter 20

"Confusion filled his senses when he awoke."

~ Ellie's Story

"Are you okay?" Brock rubbed my arms, his eyes concerned. My brain still hadn't completely pieced together what had happened. I hardly remembered anything from the past couple of minutes. Everything seemed to be a panicked blur as I watched Mikey walk to his Mustang convertible, throw open the drivers' door, and peel out of the parking lot.

My heart sagged with the weight of destructive words. Gaslighting, arrogant words of a narcissist who I knew never *truly* cared about me. He loved himself more than he could ever loved me. I squeezed my eyes shut, trying to combat the sinking feelings of guilt.

Maybe he did love me and I just kept screwing it up. Maybe if I didn't spend so much time not being okay with stuff, he'd treat me with more respect.

He's right, you know.

I sighed as Brock sat me in the booth again.

You are a tramp. Maybe you really did cheat on him.

I shook my head at that thought.

No. He cheated on me. He's the issue, not—

My fingers trembled, wracked with the torment of trying to control my thoughts as they spiraled.

"Ellie," Brock began, his voice hesitant yet firm. "Don't let him get to you. Remember that it's about him. Not you."

Brock's lying to you.

I can't trust anyone. Everyone thinks you're the one who cheated on Mikey.

"It's not me," I muttered under my breath over and over. "I didn't do anything, it's not me."

The words fell on empty ears. I didn't believe them. No one else would either. No one ever believed *me.* I was too dramatic, too sensitive, too selfish and conceited.

I looked at my wrists where his fingernails broke skin. That inadvertently brought the bloody scratches to Brock's attention. He sighed and pressed his forehead into his palm with a long groan. Self-consciously, I covered them and hung my head.

Hide them so no one will see. What will they think?

That you did it to yourself, that's what.

"What happened this time?" Brock asked, his voice muffled by the hand pressed against his mouth. He waited patiently for me to answer, though I didn't know how.

My throat tightened when I tried to swallow. I tossed my head upward, avoiding Brock's gaze and blinking frantically to hold back the tears.

"He . . . held me hostage in the booth so that I couldn't escape."

The truth of those words felt foreign and left a sour taste on my tongue. *Had he really done that? Or did I do something that upset him again?*

"I'm sorry, Brock," I muttered as my body began shaking. He sighed, gathering me to his chest.

"You have *nothing* to be sorry for."

Yes, I do. I have everything to apologize for. Did I really cheat on Mikey by spending time with Erick? Maybe I'd read into his actions too much. Maybe we really weren't broken up and I went with another guy anyway.

How could I do that to him?

No, Ellie. You guys broke up. You shouldn't feel bad for spending time with anyone you care about.

I couldn't stop the tears as they came, pouring out of me in gasps and sobs. My fingers gathered his shirt in tight fists. My body trembled uncontrollably, convulsing from the shock of what'd happened.

Confusion encompassed every piece of me until it swallowed me whole. My body felt numb to the point of unrecognition. My legs seemed like separate entities from my torso. Everything Mikey said consumed and ate at my insides until I couldn't comprehend right from wrong anymore.

Was he right?

How many times had I let him manipulate me into thinking something was my fault?

Was it my fault?

Why was I so insistent that he'd cheated on me?

Why couldn't I just spend my energy agreeing with him instead of fighting him? It was so much easier.

You're a masochist, Ellie. You look for ways to blame yourself. Why wouldn't it be your fault?

I choked on those thoughts as they crowded me at every angle like an angry mob, all protesting my existence. I crumbled beneath the heavy weight of their conflicting ideas and words.

So many *ugly* words.

"Let it out," Brock hummed, stroking my hair as he held me against his chest.

"What have I done?" I huffed, air choking from my tight throat. "I don't know what to believe anymore, Brock. I'm so confused."

"What's there to be confused about? We all know Mikey's a self-absorbed jerk who knows how to manipulate. Why care what he thinks?"

Those words pinched. Twisted and curled around the tender parts of my heart that still hoped for him. The part that wanted there to still be *some* redeemable quality. No bad guy had zero rede[illegible]ualities. Right?

[illegible]e," I whimpered, hugging him tighter.

"Why, Ellie? He's a monster—"

"I know, but—he's also my ex-boyfriend. I've seen the good in him. I know it's there."

"Ellie, he was manipulating you. There's a term for it, I'm sure. Don't expect *me* to know it, since I don't usually care about that stuff. I don't have characters to dream up."

Characters to dream up.

I thought of Erick. His pleasant, trusting smile.

What would he think if he saw me?

I stiffened uncomfortably, still keeping my arms around Brock's thin waist.

My mind flashed back to the night Mikey taught me how to play my favorite song on the guitar. How much he made me laugh with his jokes. He could make anything into something funny. And when we first started dating, he treated me like a queen. Showering me with lavish dates and gifts that I'd only dreamed about in stories.

How can you just forget that?

How could I ever let go of someone who made me feel so special?

"I know he did all that stuff. But what about looking at the positives about him? I know the guy I fell in love with is still there somewhere."

"Elle, you just got punched in the gut by a psychopath. How can you think anything but negative?"

"I know he can be . . . mean sometimes," I began, not believing a word I said. Brock scoffed and I felt him shake his head against the top of mine. "But . . . I s—still. . ."

I breathed in, the space in my stomach where he punched me aching. The pain made me wince.

Wow, that's so much worse than a corset ever was.

The pain of hopeless realization overpowered any physical pain Mikey had every caused me.

"No . . . You're right," I muttered, memories of the darkness in Mikey's eyes whenever I didn't obey his self-serving whims flashing across my vision when I blinked. "He said I'd never really be alone. What if he's been stalking me for the past eight months? How can I ever know if I'm safe? I'm not safe. I'm never safe. No matter what I do, he's there. He's *always* there. Even when I don't see him, he's in my head. Screaming at me. I can't get away from him, Brock."

I hardly noticed Lindsay ask if I was okay. When Brock asked for chef's famous pizza, I wanted nothing more to do than crumble from hunger and gratitude.

"I don't know what to do. I'm scared. I'm so *scared,"* I continued, my mouth running off without me. "What if—"

"Ellie," Brock barked, pulling me away and making me look him directly in the eyes by holding my face in his palms. "You're safe now. If he ever comes near you again, I'll be right there with an arrow pointed at his head. I'm just sorry I didn't have my bow this time."

A small bit of the burden pressing on my chest lifted and I allowed a light chuckle escape. I squeezed him closer, closing my eyes and basking in being held by someone I trusted so deeply.

"Thank you for being such a great friend, Brock," I breathed. "I'll always love you for that."

Chapter 21

"Tyral's castle towered into the sky, reaching toward the ominous light of the moon."

~ Ellie's Story

"Where do you usually write?" Erick leaned against a pillar in his chambers, one leg casually crossed over the other. My heart leaped and I whirled around to face him. I hardly remembered even going into Tyral to spend time with him. It seemed as second nature as writing now.

Yet, I couldn't get my head out of the café where Mikey had held me hostage. Punched me in the gut. Subconsciously, my fingers gripped my stomach where the corset beneath my bodice constricted the bruise. It ached with the memory.

"You've mentioned you hadn't been in the forest for some time," Erick continued when I didn't respond. "If you don't write there, where do you go?"

"Umm . . ."

It took *way* too long for my brain to connect to the present again.

"Try that again, sweetheart. . ."

Mikey's glaring scowl stuck to my subconscious as if he were there with us.

"I'll always have a right to know."

I couldn't shake away the chill rushing through my system with the memory of those words.

"Ellie?"

I flinched, waking up again from the trance I'd fallen into.

"Before my dad left, I used to write on that fallen tree all the time," I blurted too quickly.

I cringed, picking at the blue polish still clinging to my fingernails. Seeing them against the elegant, light pink dress made me feel like a little girl again, playing dress-up. I frowned, memories of mocking words prodding at my subconscious with mourning of a childhood littered with ridicule.

"Really?" Erick asked, genuinely interested. "Why'd you stop?"

Frantically, I jumped to another memory in response without looking up again . . . or thinking.

"I wrote on any paper around the house that I could find. Which was why Dad finally decided to just make a sturdy notebook for me. He and Mom probably got sick of how many trees I'd killed from using so much of their printing paper. I still write in various notebooks to get a general idea down before I use the one he gave me. After he left, I didn't really want to go back to the forest again, so I started writing at the bookstore where you and I met. It's become something of a sanctuary for me since he disappeared. We used to spend a lot of time there together, but it's a little easier than the forest. There are memories I have of him at the bookstore too. They're just less painful, ya know?"

Erick remained silent for a moment.

In horror, I realized how recklessly I'd let those words escape. I looked at him for the first time since I'd started talking. His countenance softened with an emotion I'd seen many times before in people when I talked about Dad.

"Yeah, I do. I'm sorry about your father," he said gently.

Unexpected emotion constricted my throat. So many times, I'd longed to hear those words come from him. I'd poured every emotion I felt toward Dad into him. Every second of betrayal, anger, hurt, abandonment. My need for love. Desperation. Fear. All the emotions I experienced after Dad left, Erick experienced in his own way. Hearing those words from him tugged at something inside me. Something yanked out of me, releasing an unexpected flood of anger surging through me and made my blood feel hot.

All at once, I felt the rejection of everyone around me. Every roll of my mother's eyes. Every word Mikey ever spat at me and harmful touch he forced on me. Every time Monika treated me like an incompetent little brat.

And it was all *his* fault.

If Dad hadn't left, I wouldn't have let Mikey treat me the way he did. That was just what guys did. They hurt me. They betrayed me. They didn't listen. They didn't care.

Because of *him,* Erick would *die* because he would never find someone to love. No one to say those three words to. Because he left me, I couldn't open up to Erick.

I recognized the look in Erick's eyes when he looked at me. I didn't want to, but I did. He cared about me.

Do I really want him to?

No. For my sake, I don't. For his sake, I do.

The weight of my emotions made me weak. My lungs felt constricted. The world seemed too vast. Too close. Too much at once.

I sighed, leaning against a smooth pillar for support. Trying to catch my breath through the panic rising in my stomach tightened my throat. My body felt like it weighed several tons. The slightest movement took every ounce of energy I could muster. Breathing caused me to feel like I'd run a mile in weighted shoes.

I didn't want to think anymore. I didn't want to feel. I just wanted to be devoured by numbness. It was easier than *feeling.*

"Ellie, what's wrong?" Erick asked, his hands landing on my waist as if trying to support my weight for me.

Too much, I thought. *It's too much.*

Limply, I swatted at his hands, my head falling to the side. "Stop, I'm fine."

The world swirled with the responsibility and impossibility of my position. My eyes aimlessly wandered my surroundings, purposely avoiding Erick's frantic expression.

"What happened?" His voice sounded distant in comparison to my own screaming thoughts.

You can't help him. You can't fall in love with him. He shouldn't fall in love with you anyway. You're no good for anyone, especially someone who is just going to die anyway. What were you thinking? You can't do anything to help. Never have and never will.

Please stop looking at me like you'd jump in front of a bus for me, Erick. It's not helping anything.

My legs felt rubbery. Air seemed sparse.

"I miss him," I breathed, surprising myself by the confession as I buried my face in my hands.

Erick's fingers pulled my hands away, attempting to look at my face through my hair.

"Ellie," he muttered, sounding heartbroken.

I turned away, ashamed by the tears pooling in my eyes. Pursing my lips, I hid my face from him again, shaking my head with hopelessness. With every ounce of energy, I tried pushing those emotions away. I'd done it so often before.

Who did I miss? Dad . . . or Mikey?

What was it about Erick that made me want to spread open my heart for him to see?

In spite of everything in me, every wall I'd spent so long trying to build around it, my heart longed to be part of him. He was part of me. I wanted to feel connected to *someone,* especially him.

"Ellie."

Hearing him say my name caught me off guard and I squeezed my eyes shut, forcing a smile as I turned to him. I'd practiced doing that so much, I'd nearly mastered it. With a deep inhale, I sucked in all the emotion and locked it away in the hollow void that'd been punctured into my chest the day Dad left.

The numbness soaked into my skin and I let myself absorb it wholeheartedly.

Desperate, my thoughts searched for something story related to distract me.

All that came to me was the ending. Erick's dragon form destroying the kingdom. His human form nearly nonexistent through the rage of a red dragon.

I winced. My body completely exhausted.

"Ellie, please don't dodge me anymore. It's not fair. What's wrong?" he said, brushing my hair away.

His gesture made me flinch. A dull sting in my chest like someone pricked me with a thousand fine-tipped needles. The sensation tightened my throat and burned when I swallowed the emotions threatening to make me feel again.

"I'm fine," I said firmly, stepping away from him as fast as I could. "What's not fair?"

His eyebrows pulled together, sympathy gleaming in his eyes with a caring and gentle shimmer against the light.

A mischievous smile teased his mouth.

"You're always right on the verge of showing me the girl behind those pretty, blue eyes, but you never let me really see her."

My heart raced with that and I cringed, cursing myself for making him such a smooth talker.

You're not making this any easier, buddy.

"Erick," I began, trying to control my breathing as I looked him in the eyes.

He smiled at hearing me say his name. "Yes?"

"You're dodging me now," I observed, allowing some lightheartedness back into the conversation to pierce the tension between us as he subtly leaned closer to me.

He winked playfully. "Now, how am I doing that?"

I frowned, feeling frantic with the memory of Mikey's eyes as they scanned me like he silently imagined the things he'd do to me. My skin felt sticky and gross just thinking about it.

Erick's eyes stayed locked to me, but at my face. Never wandering elsewhere.

Uncomfortably, I rubbed my arms, trying to forget the way Mikey's hands felt at the café. Instead, I was transported back in Mikey's forceful grip as he led me to the booth at The Cherry on Top. His fingernails indenting my skin. His smile as he pretended a casual nature. Erick's hands felt hot and I thought they might burn me if I let him continue holding me like that. I crumbled at the memory, shriveling away from Erick's touch like a hot iron as his fingers grazed my cheekbones.

"Don't touch me, Mikey," I screeched, trembling as I struggled, surprised when Erick immediately let go.

He held his hands up, shock on his face.

Stupid girl, you overreacted again.

I stared at him, cowering with my arms cuddled to my chest.

"Whoa, easy," Erick said, his tone lightened by a mild chuckle. "Who's Mikey?"

"M—Mikey." I muttered, dazed from the aftermath of the flashback. "He's . . . no one."

I felt as though I'd run a marathon. My stomach pinched and I winced from the pain of the bruise from Mikey's fist.

"Ow," I moaned, embarrassed by my extreme reaction and actually grateful for the distraction of pain. I stood straight again, sighing grandly as I relaxed my exhausted muscles. "Sorry. I'm a little jumpy today."

Erick hesitated, nodding as his arms seeming ready to catch me if I collapsed. "Yeah, I can see that."

He gasped unexpectedly, cringing with pain. Instantly, I jolted to attention and shot a glance toward the window. Dusk barely inched over the horizon.

The brighter the moon, the earlier his curse will begin.

Chapter 22

"It seemed that the most real thing in the world was what seemed completely illogical."

~ *Ellie's Story*

Erick brought me back through an alleyway between the village and palace walls. Its stone smelled dusty and ancient. Vines grew between the cracks, tangling around each other with small flowers intertwined between the rocks. I followed him close. I heard his breath. His hands trembled and tightened into fists as scales slithered across his backhand.

His change approached quickly.

The mouth of the alleyway came into view and Erick stopped, leaning against the stone with a grunt. My heart ached seeing him in pain.

"How close are you?" I asked.

Erick grimaced, squeezing his side as he gazed out the opening. "Too close."

"Let's go then," I said, moving around him. As I passed, he turned around and I realized how close the stone walls crammed together. My heart leaped when his eyes met mine, closer than I'd anticipated. His shoulder brushed against mine, his physical presence registering in my consciousness for seemingly the first time.

He still seemed so distant, like a dream. Close enough to touch, but too far to ever reach. Everything in me wanted him to be more than a dream. My breath caught in my throat as my eyes drifted over his features. Every little thing about him drew me in. Eventually, my gaze landed on my hand resting on his shoulder as it involuntarily slid to his chest. His breath quickened and I felt his heartbeat leap through clothes, pounding in time with mine.

"How can you feel so real?" I breathed dazedly.

The words weren't intended to be spoken aloud, yet I didn't regret their escape. My heart jumped into my throat as I breathed in every detail of him. The palpable air around us felt thick with tension. My fingers extended, tangling with the fabric of his cravat. The amethyst jewels sewn into its hem glittered. His Adam's apple moved when he swallowed, his lips parted slightly, eyes downcast before finding mine and holding tightly. The world swayed around us, every movement slow and savored.

"Do you still think I'm a dream?" he whispered, his focus flashing toward my lips.

His fingers brushed across my cheek, tucking my hair behind my hair. My heart thrashed when he leaned in toward me. My brain didn't register what was happening until his nose skimmed the tip of mine and his breath tickled my skin.

A sharp intake of breath yanked me back to reality. Blinking hard, I let go of his cravat and stepped back, bowing away from him. The emotion in Erick's deep expression wounded a part of me. He reached for me as I left, confusion in his eyes. Their silver iris lined with crimson.

I frowned and turned away.

"What's wrong?" he asked, brushing his hand over my arm.

I shriveled away from his touch, rubbing at the goosebumps risen to the surface.

"Nothing," I said simply, not wanting to elaborate.

He winced, dropping his hand with an embarrassed chuckle. "I'm sorry," he muttered. "I shouldn't have taken the liberty. I just. . ."

I watched him, anticipating the ending of that sentence. My gaze briefed his hands under the sleeve of his tunic to see the scales forming.

"I don't know what came over me," he continued.

It wasn't you, I thought, giving him a reassuring smile through the flurry of emotions twirling in my stomach. *You wouldn't feel anything toward me anyway.*

His brow furrowed and he glanced out the alleyway opening. Sighing, he looked skyward at the setting sun.

"Not again," he grumbled, rubbing the scales growing on his cheek. "Follow me, I'll take you home."

He took my hand. As an initial reaction, I jerked it away, hugging my torso.

Flinching, he frowned. "I'm sorry."

Erick ducked through the mouth of the alleyway. I followed close behind until we reached the field outside the kingdom walls. The mood between us changed as I walked with folded arms, keeping a safe distance from him.

He walked with his head down, a frown prominent in contrast to the joy that'd been on his face most of the day. My heart sank with guilt when I saw the forlorn sadness darkening his features. He maneuvered around branches, stumps, and a rock gracefully, as opposed to me, hiking up my skirts probably farther than was proper.

The song of sparrows rang through the trees, creating a serene atmosphere I otherwise would've relished in. But in that moment, it felt as melancholy as a mourning dove.

Erick didn't speak, but kept glancing skyward every so often, the scales on his cheeks slowly spreading onto his neck. He winced, groaning as he rubbed his side.

"You okay?" I asked, placing a stabilizing hand on his back.

He tensed under my touch, stopping to bend forward. His breath huffed from his nostrils and he moaned. When he met my gaze, his eyes were red, the silver scales on his face and neck blended with scales the shade of blood.

"Fine," he spat, coughing and gripping his side. "Go ahead, I can't keep going."

I shook my head in defiance. I wanted to be there with him through his transition. I wanted to help him. Somehow make it less painful. Why? Probably a guilty conscience.

"You're not getting rid of me that easily, Erick."

His laugh ripped through his throat in a raspy coughing fit as he doubled over.

"You're not fine," I said, trying to ease him to the ground slowly. He resisted, straightening his spine with a face scrunched up in pain.

"No," he grunted, his hand landing firmly on my shoulder, catching me off guard. He looked me in the eyes. Perspiration beaded on his temples and his eyes were heavy and distant as if from lack of sleep. He almost looked like Mikey after a party.

My eyebrows pulled together sympathetically. His mouth flickered with a half-hearted smile. He leaned forward, planting a swift kiss on my cheek before he grimaced, his grip digging briefly into my arm in an effort to suppress his pain.

"Go." He let go, pushing himself back as scales slithered over his tense hands and his fingernails grew into talons.

Dazed, I stumbled backward.

What just happened?

My chest hurt with empathy and guilt. After a moment of confused hesitation, I obeyed, gathering my skirts and sprinting toward the Enchanted Arbor as the agonizing screeches of a man turned monster rang out.

I did that to him. He was in pain because of me. And there wasn't anything I could do about it.

As I crossed back into Taylor's Grove, all I could think about was how I would reverse this. Rewrite history to save him from himself.

And that kiss.

Chapter 23

"The ground beneath him felt cold and unforgiving as it dragged him forward."

~ Ellie's Story

That night, I lie on my back in bed, wishing it would suck me in. I wondered if it would, depending on how long I could remain still. A burden heavily sat on my chest and seemed to push me further and further until I hoped I would be swallowed up.

Where was the pounding in my heart coming from? I didn't like it. If it was something I should've enjoyed, I didn't.

I didn't want to think of Erick as anything but the fictional character in a book I'd written. I didn't want to believe he was real. Yet everything in me hoped he was. I wanted the fantasy of his kiss to be real. I wanted to imagine that he actually wanted to kiss me. Not just because he was on the verge of change, but because he cared about me.

I knew that wasn't true though. He only needed me around to figure out how to help him break his curse. He didn't really care about *me.*

I didn't want to know if the things I'd written would actually happen. That wasn't a responsibility I wanted. If I had, I wouldn't have caused so much pain. I wouldn't have made Erick's curse so excruciating for him. Why did I do that to him?

Because you didn't think you'd actually be hurting a real person. He was just a character before, remember?

A shiver rolled over my skin with dread and I sat up.

I'd potentially harmed an entire kingdom of people for the sake of a good story.

I wanted to read what I'd written. Maybe I hadn't done anything too drastic. Maybe people wouldn't get hurt. Maybe people wouldn't die.

Maybe Erick's dragon wouldn't really change him forever.

Frantic, grabbing my notebook at the side of my bed, scrambling for any clues. The light of the moon through my curtains provided little light, making it difficult to see anything. Glancing toward my door, I thought of turning on my lamp.

Monika slept in the room across from me. If she hadn't complained so often of my lamp waking her up in the middle of the night, I would've done it. The last thing I wanted to do was wake *her* up.

It wasn't worth the risk.

I sighed, reluctantly snapping my notebook shut and throwing myself back onto my bed to think.

Lifting my hand in front of me, I examined the details in my fingers, palms, and wrists, remembering how Erick's hand felt in mine for the instant he held it. Somehow, that memory calmed me.

What's wrong with me?

Monika's words repeated in my mind as they often did.

I don't think you're capable of learning, Ellie.

Something in me shifted with that memory. Numbed my senses.

As I rubbed my knuckles in silence, I stared at the ceiling, trying to think of anything else.

What was I supposed to do when my automatic response to boredom and contemplation was thinking of Erick? Trying not to think of him and his story in those moments had become a futile attempt and nearly impossible to avoid. He dominated every aspect of my life, but I loved that about him. He and his story felt like what gave me life when I felt lifeless.

What would I do if I ever lost that?

How would I handle it if he broke my heart?

Who am I kidding? He'd never see me that way. If he did, it wouldn't last. He didn't do long-term relationships. Never has, probably never will. Why waste my time thinking about it?

Why am I even thinking about it? He's my character. Just because he's real doesn't mean anything productive will ever happen between us in the relationship category.

It can't *happen. He's cursed and I'm emotionally unavailable. It won't happen. Because I won't let it.*

My fingers brushed across my cheek where he'd kissed me then came to rest on my lips.

He'd nearly kissed me.

Normally, I'd imagine any other girl in the world giggling, sighing, and holding her hand to her heart at the memory of something like that.

I, however, felt terrified at the prospect.

If I could've erased the way I felt around him, I would've. I knew how Erick fell in love. He was reckless and passionate. I didn't need that, yet everything about it lured me closer to him. He didn't understand why girls were drawn to him. He only enjoyed it as it happened, falling very quickly and carelessly.

I bit my lips, reminded of his heartbeat against my fingers. I wished my own heart hadn't gotten so carried away in the moment with him. I groaned, rolling over and tugging my favorite purple pillow to my chest.

Pepper hopped onto the side of the bed, making a small grunt when she landed. A calming purr erupted from her throat as she thrust her head against the back of my hand, begging for attention. I smiled, stroking her soft fur. She arched her back, purring louder as she flopped onto her side, pressing herself close to me. Her eyes closed when I scratched her ear, an expression bright with contentment. Her black and gray striped fur felt soft, though a bit matted from old age.

"What have I gotten myself into, Pepper?" I asked.

She looked up at me, rubbing her chin across my arm. I smiled, rolling toward her and petting her with both hands. Something about having a cat calmed any anxiety I experienced.

For the thousandth time since it happened, my thoughts wandered to the kiss he'd given my cheek. The way my heart skipped at the memory frightened me. I didn't expect it, certainly. But what was even more surprising to me was the skittish way my heart palpitated because of it.

I sighed through my nose. I'd never felt so depressed or so excited about the prospect of someone before. Expectations came with the feelings I experienced that day. I didn't want those. If I gave into them, I was afraid I'd fall too fast again then end up alone and cold in the end.

I needed to avoid that at all costs.

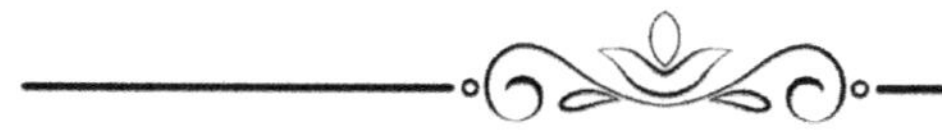

End of Book 1

Acknowledgments

First and foremost, I'd like to thank my Lord and Savior, Jesus Christ, and my Heavenly Father for creating so many miracles in my life that led to me finishing this novel over the past ten years. They gave me all the talents and circumstances that made it possible.

I couldn't have written this book without the help of my beyond wonderful hubby, Ryan. He's supported me in everything from the beginning to end. He's believed in me when I didn't and he helped reawaken my passion for writing in the best way possible with his supportive, positive attitude.

My mom, Lorena Wilson, spent countless hours and dollars involving me in every teen writing conference and critique group she could. Her dedication and belief helped mold me into who I am today.

Jessica Dixon, my best friend since we were twelve-years-old, pushed and encouraged me to write when I didn't want to and is one of my biggest supports in more ways than one. I wouldn't be the person I am today if it weren't for her. She was so amazing to be my cover artist and she rocks at it!

Kendra Bitton for being a huge supporter of this story by always being willing to listen to me read it during our long phone calls when we were younger. It helped more than she'll ever know.

Emily Bingham has always been an inspiration to be because of her astonishing drive to accomplish whatever goal she sets her mind to. She inspires me to be more than I was.

I have to give a shout-out to all my critique group friends! They always faithfully read every version of this story in particular and encouraged me to keep growing and getting better, not only in my writing but as a person.

Margot Hovley, who's the greatest writing mentor/teacher I ever could've asked for.

Shanna Hovley, for always being so amazingly positive and encouraging, yet honest with every critique she's ever given.

Michaella Micham, who's sweet and wonderful positivity helps me through a lot of dark edits that would've drowned me otherwise.

Conner Cluff, for always keeping my characters entertaining and interesting and making me laugh when I didn't feel like it.

Kiara Horowitz, for helping me create well-rounded characters that could be lovable for other people besides me.

Knight Taylor, for giving logical and uplifting advice any time I gave him a piece I'd created, whether it was writing or a drawing.

Lastly, I want to thank my celebrity hero, Taylor Swift for being such a huge force of inspiration, not only through her music but also for simply being the genuine person she is. Her music video for her song, *Love Story,* was a huge driving force for inspiration while writing this series.

Chandler R. Williamson

The Story Behind "Beyond My Words"

I started writing this book when I was about thirteen-years-old. I'd spent a lot of years drawing characters and creating little short stories with my friend, Kendra, before realizing I wanted to be an author someday. I wrote one other story before *Beyond My Words,* that will come to fruition at some future point. But when I thought of *Beyond My Words,* I knew I'd be hooked for life.

I was sitting on the top bunk of my bunk bed, listening to the song, *Unwritten,* by Natasha Bedingfield while drawing a picture of some random girl. When it occurred to me that a story might be hidden inside that girl, I had the tagline, "What if everything you wrote about came to life?" enter my thoughts. I latched onto that idea like nothing else and held onto it with both hands.

My mind swirled with a thousand different questions, many of which are still relevant in the final version of the book you read today. Probably the biggest concepts that stuck were Ellie being in high school, Jennica and Brock's relationship, and Erick's curse turning him into a red dragon. I hadn't done any research into dragons at the time, but, for some reason, I just knew he would be.

This story has changed *drastically* over the years, one of those changes being that Ellie's name was originally Adrian, nicknamed Adrie.

Erick used to have a girlfriend and go to Ellie's school. That concept wouldn't work now since Erick is now 21 and Ellie is 18. That girlfriend ended up being meshed with Jennica's character.

There used to be a purple stone called the Lilac Fire I used as the source of all magic that ended up being meshed in with Ellie's notebook and Petegrath's scepter.

Mikey didn't used to be the main antagonist of the book, but it used to be Erick's step-father, Hadrian. Eventually, however, I merged their characters to create the bad guy who makes everyone I've seen read this book shudder and cringe with his lustful and creepy behavior.

This book used to be purely contemporary until I saw Taylor Swift's music video for her song, *Love Story.* I fell completely in love with it and, from that moment on, I knew I would write a fantasy novel. To this day, it remains my favorite song.

Most of the inspiration I received for Mikey stemmed from the music video for, yet another Taylor Swift song, *I Knew You Were Trouble.*

There are a lot of Taylor Swift references hidden in this story, if you know to look for them. One of those Easter Eggs is the way all my characters hold a pen between their index and middle fingers. All my characters have this trait, no matter the story. Another one is Ellie's birthday being December 13th, shared by Taylor. Ellie's dress in the end of the book is meant to be a mixture of the two dresses that Taylor wears in the *Love Story* music video as well as the dress from Disney's live action *Cinderella.*

A lot of things in this book are personal to me, but any views, situations, and/or opinions expressed in this book are purely coincidental. Each character has unique viewpoints and characteristics that may or may not resemble real events, but it is purely coincidence. I don't seem to have much control over these characters since they understand that they are the writers of their own stories.

For years, I've slaved over trying to control what these characters do, but they all have their own ideas of who they are and what their roles in the story are. Whenever I tried controlling them to be the way I wanted them to be, it would often come across completely wrong and I'd be left being essentially beaten into the ground with criticism. Until I let loose and really got to know each character individually, I realized how much I didn't know about them. It wasn't until I allowed them to create the story for me that I realized how beautifully unique my creations in this series are.

I could not be prouder of who I've discovered in each of them and I love these characters so much more now than I ever have before.

I hope you enjoyed reading this novel and getting to know my characters. I hope you've fallen in love with them as much as I have. These characters have been such a huge part of my life for the past eleven years. They really have come to life for me, though I hope I'm *never* faced with Erick's dragon form like Ellie was.

Thank you so much for reading my novel and I hope you'll continue on to read Book 2 of *Beyond My Words.*

Love,
Chandler R. Williamson

If you liked what you read, check out these other books by Chandler R. Williamson

Convicted: 25 to Life

The Holiday Spirit

The Miracle:
A Latter-Day Tale

Look for Book 2 of Beyond My Words

October 2020

Follow Chandler R. Williamson on Social Media

Facebook: Tyral Books & Customs

Twitter: ChandlerRWilli2

Instagram: Chandler.R.Williamson

Blog: AuthorChandlerRWilliamson.com

Check out some of her other works and custom crafts

Etsy: TyralBooksAndCustoms

Made in the USA
Middletown, DE
07 July 2022